Carbonel

'I believe you want me to follow you'

BARBARA SLEIGH

Carbonel
THE KING OF THE CATS

Illustrated by
V. H. Drummond

THE NEW YORK REVIEW CHILDREN'S COLLECTION
New York

Published in the United States of America by
The New York Review of Books, 1755 Broadway, New York, NY 10019

Distributed to the Trade by Publishers Group West

A catalog record for this book is available from the Library of Congress

Cover design by Louise Fili Ltd

Printed in the United States on acid-free paper.
10 9 8 7 6 5 4 3 2 1

November 2004
www.nyrb.com

Contents

To

FABIA

and the whiskered shades of

TIBBY

TARQUIN

QUINCE

and

SPIKE

I

Breaking-up

ROSEMARY'S satchel bounced cheerfully up and down on her back as she hopped on and off the pavement of Tottenham Grove. She enjoyed school, except for arithmetic and boiled fish on Fridays. But breaking-up, as you will have noticed, even if you have not particularly distinguished yourself, gives everyone a delightful party feeling, particularly at the end of the Summer Term. Rosemary Brown was fizzing with it as she bounced up and down on the kerb.

She had just reached the pillar box at the corner when Mary Winters came by with her friend Arlene.

'Hallo, Rosie!' said Mary, 'we're going to Blackpool tomorrow!'

'Blackpool is common, my auntie says. We're going to Bournemouth.' Arlene wore brooches, and sometimes a gold bracelet to go to school, although it was not allowed. Her auntie thought a great many things were common. 'Where are you going, Rosie?'

Rosemary hopped off the kerb, changed feet, and hopped on again with great deliberation.

'Nowhere!' she said as carelessly as she could manage.

'Poor thing!' said Arlene with maddening pity, and the two friends hurried off, giggling, together.

Rosemary went on doggedly hopping, but the party feeling was only fizzing at half-cock now. Mary and Arlene knew quite well that she was unlikely to be going away. It was hard enough for her mother to manage at all, because she had no money but her widow's pension, and what she earned by sewing for people. Rosemary stopped hopping. Her satchel was beginning to hurt when she bounced. It was heavy because it was full of end of term things, a rather squashy piece of clay modelling, her indoor shoes and a dirty overall, as well as some books. She ran the rest of the way down Tottenham Grove with her short pigtails flapping up and down sideways, like the blades of an old pair of scissors.

Rosemary and her mother lived at number ten, in three furnished rooms on the top floor, with use of bath on Tuesdays and Fridays, and a share of the kitchen. It was not a very pleasant arrangement, because the furniture was ugly (most of it was covered with horse-hair that pricked, even through a winter tunic), and the bathroom was always festooned with other people's washing. But it was cheap, and would have to do until they could find somewhere unfurnished, and then they would be able to use their own comfortable, shabby belongings again.

The houses in Tottenham Grove were all exactly alike, very tall and thin, with a great deal of peeling paint and cracking plaster. Once they had been rather grand, with servants in the basement, and carriages driving up to the front doors, and ladies with very large hats and very small waists paying calls. Her mother had told her all about it. But Rosie was not bothering her head about that at the moment. She knew without looking which was number ten, and went running up the twelve steps so quickly that she bumped into Mrs Walker, the landlady, who was slapping the door mat against one of the pillars of the peeling portico.

'I'm so sorry, Mrs Walker!' said Rosemary breathlessly.

'I should think so!' said Mrs Walker sourly. 'Home for the holidays? How long is it this time?'

'Six weeks,' said Rosie.

'Well, I don't know! Six weeks? I should have thought a great girl like you could have been doing something useful.'

She flopped the still dusty mat into its place, and Rosie went slowly upstairs with her satchel bumping on each step as it trailed behind her. When she opened the door of the sitting room she saw that the table was drawn up to the window and already laid.

'Mummy, what a lovely dinner!'

'Well, it's the first day of the holidays,' said her mother cheerfully, 'and I've just got three weeks' work from Mrs Pendlebury Parker, so I thought we would celebrate.'

There was a bunch of marigolds in the centre of the blue and white table cloth, a constellation of small, glowing suns. There were crescent rolls, tinned tongue and salad, and a bottle of bright pink fizzy stuff for Rosemary.

'There is ice-cream with stewed fruit afterwards,' said her mother, 'but hang up your things and wash first.'

'Tell me about Mrs Pendlebury Parker!' said Rosemary when her knife and fork began to move a little more slowly. 'Is it nice sort of sewing, and can you bring it home with you?'

Stories of Mrs Pendlebury Parker and the splendours of Tussocks, her house which was just outside the town, were always a source of wonder to Rosemary.

'I'm afraid I shall have to go there every day for the next three weeks,' said her mother. 'I'm so sorry to have to leave you for so long on your own, Poppet, but she does pay so well, I felt I could not afford to say no. I'm afraid it is largely mending linen, so I can't bring the work home.'

Rosie let the blob of ice-cream on her tongue melt completely before she answered, and then she said as cheerfully as she could, 'I shan't mind really, I expect. How hateful for you to be sides-to-middling sheets, when you ought to be making beautiful dresses!'

Mrs Brown smiled. 'Never mind, darling. Think of all the things I shall have to tell you when I come home in the evenings!'

'And perhaps,' said Rosemary brightening, 'you'll be rich enough afterwards to buy one of those things for making your sewing machine go by electricity, and then you'll earn so much more money that we shall be able to go and live somewhere else, where your ladies will come to you, instead of you having to go to their houses whatever the weather is like. And I shall dress in black satin and say, "This way, Modom!"' Her mother laughed.

'And I shall be able to say, "Mrs Pendlebury Parker," I shall say, "No, I'm afraid I cannot make you twelve flannel nightdresses by the day after tomorrow. I never sew anything coarser than crêpe de chine!"' They both laughed a great deal, and the meal ended quite cheerfully.

When they had finished, Mrs Brown had to go into the town to match some silks, so Rosemary cleared away and washed up the dinner plates. Next she put away her school things and changed into a cotton frock, and all the time she was wondering what she could do with herself for the next three weeks. Could she really do something useful, she wondered, as Mrs Walker had suggested? It had been rather unfair to call her a 'great girl', because she was rather small for her ten years. All the same, it would be wonderful, she thought, to earn some money without her mother knowing anything about it, and at the end of the holidays carelessly to pour a shower of clinking coins into her astonished lap!

'The trouble is, I don't know what I could do,' she said to herself. 'I can't sew well enough. The only thing I can do is to keep our rooms clean and tidy. I always do that in the holidays when Mummy is busy. I *can* sweep and polish and wash-up.'

She rather liked the idea, and by the time she had done up the difficult button at the back of her cotton frock Rosemary had made up her mind. She would go out daily and clean.

Now she had a hazy idea that it would be necessary to take her tools with her, in the same way that her mother took her own thimble, needles, and scissors when she went out to sew. Dusters and a scrubbing brush would be easy, but Mrs Walker would not let her past the front door with a broom without going into a long explanation, and then it would no longer be a surprise.

'Well, there is nothing for it,' she said to herself, 'I shall have to buy one for myself.'

After much rattling and poking with a dinner knife her money-box produced two and fivepence three farthings.

'P'r'aps if I went to Fairfax Market I could find a cheap broom,' she thought doubtfully. 'It's rather a long way, but I think I could get there and back before tea time.'

2

Fairfax Market

ROSEMARY put the money in her pocket and left a note for her mother; then she started off for Fairfax Market. This was held in the old part of the town in the cobbled market square. Because she imagined that two and five-pence three farthings was not very much money with which to buy a broom, she decided not to waste any of it on a bus.

She started resolutely off, only stopping occasionally to look in a shop window. But it was hot and dusty going. The pavements seemed to toast the soles of her feet through the rubber soles of her sandals. To make matters worse, one of the buckles came off. By the time she reached the market a slight drizzle was falling, and the clock on the Market Hall roof was striking four. Instead of the cheerful racket of people shouting their wares, of laughter and bustle, the stall-holders were already packing up. Rosemary went up to a stout woman who was stacking crockery which had been displayed on the cobbles.

'Please,' she said anxiously, 'will you tell me where I can buy a broom?'

'You can't,' snapped the fat woman without looking up. 'Not now you can't.' Then she straightened herself with a grunt and looked at Rosemary's disappointed face.

'Never ask a favour of a fat woman when she's bending,' she said more kindly. 'Leastways, not if you want a civil answer. Don't they teach you that at school?'

Rosie shook her head, and the fat woman went on, 'The market's been closing at four on Mondays these last three 'undred years, leastways, so my old father told me. Never mind, cheer up, lovey! 'Ave a fancy milk jug for your ma instead?'

Rosemary shook her head again and went sadly on between the rows of dismantled stalls and piles of goods hidden under tarpaulins, already glistening with rain. The money in her hand was hot and sticky, but there was nothing to buy with it, let alone a broom, so she put it back in her pocket. She inquired again of a young man who was loading bales of brightly coloured material into an ancient car.

'Please, do you know where I can buy a broom?'

But all he said was ' 'Op it, see!' So Rosemary 'opped it.

She wandered on among the drifting straw and bits of paper till she came to the end of the market, where the pavement began again. Here she found a little shop that sold newspapers and sweets and odds and ends, so she stopped to look in the window. She wondered whether to buy a toffee-apple or a liquorice bootlace to sustain her on the way home. The toffee-apple would last longer, but on the other hand she could eat a bit of the bootlace and use the rest as a skipping rope and still eat it later. She had just decided on the apple, because you cannot skip comfortably with a buckle off your sandal, when she felt something damp and furry rubbing against her bare legs. She looked down, and saw a huge black cat. Now Rosemary liked cats. If only Mrs Walker had allowed it she would certainly have had one of her own, so she bent down to stroke him. But the cat ran off and then sat down a few yards away and looked at her. Rosemary followed and tried to stroke him again, but the creature darted off for a few feet as before, and sat down to wash its paws. Rosemary laughed.

'I believe you want me to follow you! All right, I will. I'm coming!' So they went off in fits and starts, with Rosemary trying to catch the cat, who lolloped away as soon as she was within stroking distance. But although the cat did not laugh as she did, it was perfectly obvious that he was enjoying the joke as much as she was. She was just going to make a successful grab at him when she bumped into someone. It was an old woman.

'I'm so sorry!' said Rosemary.

'And so you should be,' said the old woman sharply, 'keeping me waiting like this. Well, it's yours for two and fivepence, and it's cheap at the price.'

'What is?' asked Rosemary in a puzzled way.

'The broom, of course! That's what you've come for, isn't it? If that cat is trying to fool me just because I'm going out of business...'

The cat was patting a drifting piece of orange paper with deep concentration.

'Oh, but I do want a broom!' said Rosemary eagerly.

'I've sold my stock and bought myself a new hat,' went on the old woman unexpectedly. 'How do you like it?'

Rosemary hoped she would not be asked to give an opinion about any of the rest of the old woman's clothes. The hat was certainly very fashionable. It was sprinkled with sequins and had a little veil. But perched on the old woman's wild grey hair it only served to make the hair look wilder and her ragged clothes more disreputable.

'It's very pretty,' said Rosemary. 'But shall I take off the price label? It's hanging down behind.'

'Oh, no you don't!' said the old woman fiercely. 'I paid nineteen and elevenpence for my hat and I'm not giving away any of the trimmings! You can have the broom and the cat, too, if you like, but my trimmings aren't in the bargain.'

Rosemary felt quite indignant at the turn the conversation was taking and she answered with some spirit.

'Of course I don't want the trimmings from your hat! But I wish I could have the cat.' She looked at the handsome animal who was sitting with his tail neatly curled round his feet, apparently fast asleep.

The old woman chuckled.

'He's a deep one, he is!' She paused, looked sharply at Rosemary and added, 'He's worth his weight in ... farthings.'

'But if the broom costs two and fivepence I've only got three farthings left, and he must be worth much more than that!' Surely Mrs Walker could be talked round? Anyway, she knew that her mother would not mind. It was more than likely that the queer old woman was not a very kind mistress. Rosemary had a feeling that the cat was not really asleep, but was listening with all his ears.

'You can have him for three farthings if that is all you've got,' said the old woman.

'I'll have him!' she answered breathlessly. As she said it, the cat opened his eyes, flashed one golden glance at her, and closed them again.

Rosemary pulled the money out of her pocket and put it into the not too clean hand which the old woman was already greedily holding out for it. She counted eagerly, but it was the farthings that seemed to interest her most. She held them up to her short-sighted eyes, then she bit them and chuckled.

'I guessed as much. You're in luck, my boy. Three queens for a prince!'

'They are my Queen Victoria farthings. That's why I kept them. They are all I have. Will they do?'

'Oh, aye, they'll do better than you know,' replied the old woman.

The cat was not pretending to sleep now. He was wide awake and staring at Rosemary with his two great golden eyes. 'You can take him,' she went on, and prodded him with her foot. 'And don't say I never did you a good turn, my boy. Though, mind you, it's only half undone.'

The Market Hall clock struck five as she spoke.

'It's getting awfully late,' said Rosemary. 'I think I must be going. Please may I have the broom?'

'The broom? Oh, aye, here you are.' And so saying the old woman pushed it into Rosemary's hand, turned and disappeared down a dark alley at the side of the sweet shop. As she went under the arch she ducked her head as if she was used to a much taller kind of hat.

Rosemary watched her go. Then she looked down at the broom, and her heart sank. It was not what she wanted at all. It was the sort of broom that gardeners use – a rough wooden handle with a bundle of twigs bound on at one end, and only a few dilapidated twigs at that.

'What a shame!' said Rosemary. As the full extent of her bad luck dawned on her she could not stop the hot tears from trickling down her face. The broom was useless, at least for her purpose. She had no money left to buy another, and to crown it all she would have to walk all the way home without a buckle on her shoe, with not even the consolation of a toffee-apple. However, she was a brave girl, and in the absence of a handkerchief she wiped her eyes with the back of her hand and decided to make the best of it. But just at that moment, quite clearly and distinctly, the cat said:

'It's a better bargain than it looks, you know.'

'Who said that?' Rosemary could not believe her ears.

'Me, of course!' said the cat. 'Oh, yes, of course I can talk. All animals can, but you can only hear me because you are holding the witch's broom.'

Rosemary dropped it hurriedly. Then, realizing that she could not hear the cat talk without it, she picked it up again.

'And I should treat it with respect,' went on the animal dryly. 'There's not much life in the poor thing or she would not have sold it so cheap. Trust her for that! Pity you didn't hear some of the things I said to her just now!' he went on with satisfaction. 'Not names; that is vulgar, but I tickled her up nicely!' and his tail twitched at the memory.

Rosemary remembered how the queer old woman had known, without being told, exactly how much money she had.

'But is she really a witch?' she whispered in an awed voice.

'Hush!' said the cat, hurriedly looking over his shoulder. 'Best not to use that word. She was, right up to the moment when you bought me and the broom. Now she's retired; says she's going to turn respectable.' He added scornfully, 'A fish might as well say it's decided not to swim. You haven't such a thing as a saucer of milk about you?'

Rosemary shook her head. 'Pity. YOU-KNOW-WHAT have their uses. SHE could always produce a saucer of milk no matter where we were, in the middle of

Salisbury Plain or playing catch as catch can with the Northern Lights.'

'That was kind of her, anyway,' said Rosemary.

'Not so very,' said the cat. 'If she was in a bad temper, which she generally was, like as not it would be sour.'

'Well, as soon as we get home you shall have as much milk as you can drink. But I'm afraid we shall have to walk. I haven't any money for a bus fare. Besides, I don't know whether they let cats go on buses.'

'Then go by broom,' said the cat.

'By broom?' said Rosemary, feeling rather puzzled.

'I wish you wouldn't keep repeating everything,' snapped the cat. 'Mind you, it won't fly very high. You couldn't expect it, not in the state the poor old thing is in now. But it will take us there all right. Well, go on, why don't you mount?'

'Mount?' said Rosemary.

'There you go again! It is quite simple. You just stand astride it and say where you want to go. Best do it in rhyme. It is more polite, and the poor thing is sensitive now it is so old.'

'There is not much to rhyme with ten Tottenham Grove, top floor,' said Rosemary doubtfully.

'Leave it to me,' said the cat. 'Tottenham Grove ... stove ... mauve ... I've got it. Not very polished, but it will serve. Now then, mount and hold tight!'

He balanced himself delicately on the twiggy part of the broom. 'Now repeat after me!' ...

> *Through window wide and not the door,*
> *Ten Tottenham Grove, the topmost floor!*

As Rosemary repeated it there was a faint quiver in the handle of the broom, and it rose slowly a couple of feet from the ground, wheeled sharply round, so that Rosemary nearly fell off, and went steadily on in the direction of Tottenham Grove. On it went, ignoring traffic lights, skimming zebra crossings, and leaving a train of astonished pedestrians in its wake. At first Rosemary could do nothing but shut her eyes and clutch the handle and pray that she would not fall off. But the motion was smooth and pleasant and she became aware that the cat was telling her something, so she opened her eyes.

'I ... I'm afraid I did not hear what you said.'

'I was saying,' said the cat, 'that you should always point your broom in the direction in which you want to go. I knew a young witch once who was thrown.'

'Goodness!' said Rosemary. 'What did she do?'

'Nothing. There was not much she could do. It got clean away. Nasty things, runaway brooms, apart from the expense of getting a new one, and the trouble of breaking it in.'

By now Rosemary was beginning to enjoy herself. She knew that cars were not supposed to do more than thirty miles an hour when driving through a town, and as they steadily overtook everything else on the road she said to herself: 'Perhaps it doesn't apply to witch's brooms.'

A policeman outside the Town Hall tried to hold them up before he realized what she was riding. His astonishment when he did realize so staggered him that he quite lost his head, and the traffic jam that resulted gave Rosemary a clear road to the corner of Tottenham Grove.

When they neared number ten she had enough sense to hold on for all she was worth. The broom gathered itself together for a tremendous effort, rose steeply, swooped into her bedroom window, and collapsed exhausted on the floor. Rosemary stood up and rubbed her elbow. Then she picked up the broom again.

'Best hide it in the wardrobe,' said the cat.

'Thank you, Broom!' she whispered, and stood it in the corner behind her winter coat. She could hear her mother using the sewing machine next door.

3

Carbonel

'HALLO, darling!' said Mrs Brown. 'How late you are. I didn't hear you come upstairs.'

'I'm sorry I'm late,' burst out Rosemary, 'but Mummy, I've bought a cat in the Market. Please may I keep him?'

Mrs Brown rubbed her forehead with the back of her hand in the way she had when she was tired and worried.

'A cat? Oh dear! Of course I don't mind. But Mrs Walker isn't very pleased with us at the moment.'

'Because of the toffee?' said Rosemary, rather crestfallen. 'I'd forgotten about that. Besides, that was three weeks ago, and I never meant to let it boil over. This isn't an ordinary cat, he talks! Don't you, my Pussums?'

The black cat yawned disdainfully, jumped on to the window sill, and gazed abstractedly out.

'I forgot. You can only hear him talk if you are holding the witch's broom-stick.'

Her mother was smiling in a grown-up 'Bless-your-little-fancies' way. Then she laughed.

'He might really have been showing you that he doesn't approve of being called Pussums. Poor creature, he is terribly thin. You had better give him that bit of fish in the meat-safe. I was going to make some fish-cakes, for supper, but we can open a tin of something instead.'

Rosemary beamed. She knew that if her mother began to take an interest in the cat she would never have

23

the heart to turn him away – at least, not without a struggle. The cat ate the fish and drank a saucer of milk and then, purring deeply, turned his attention to his appearance. He washed his paws and whiskers very thoroughly while Rosemary, curled up on the horse-hair sofa, ate the tea her mother had kept for her. There was a mug of milk, some jam sandwiches, and a piece of Swiss roll.

'He is really a very handsome animal,' went on her mother. 'You know, Mrs Pendlebury Parker never found her ginger cat again, although she offered a reward for him. It must be four months now since she lost him.'

'The one she called Popsey Dinkums?' asked Rosemary. She was busy unwinding her Swiss roll, a fascinating occupation which was only allowed at picnic sort of meals.

'Mrs Parker thought the world of that animal,' went on her mother. 'I've seen it eating meals I would willingly have had for our supper. Oh dear, why does the shuttle always have to give out just a few inches from the end of the seam? I must finish this dressing-gown for Miss Withers before I start working for Mrs Pendlebury Parker.'

'And that means tonight. Poor Mummy!'

Mrs Brown sighed. 'Never mind. You had better get to bed early, Rosie. You are yawning your head off! We will talk to Mrs Walker in the morning about the cat, but don't be too hopeful, darling.'

'I am rather tired. I expect it was all that walking this afternoon. But Mummy, can I have him to sleep in my room? I'm sure he'll be good, won't you, Pussums? And if he wants to go out there is always the little flat roof outside my window.'

'Well, really,' said her mother, 'he might be trying to get round me!' She bent down to stroke the cat, who was rubbing himself against her legs and purring loudly. 'Very well, dear, he can sleep with you if you like.'

Later that evening, when she had kissed her mother good night and put on her nightdress, Rosemary fetched the broom from her wardrobe, jumped on to her bed, and patted the quilt beside her.

'Come on, Pussums! Now we can have a long talk.'

'Not if you call me by that revolting name. Pussums indeed! As if I were a common or garden, mousing, sit-by-the-fire cat.'

'I'm very sorry, Pu ... I mean, what shall I call you, then?'

'You may call me Carbonel. That is my name.'

The cat had jumped up beside her and was kneading the quilt with his front paws, before settling in the hollow she had made in the bedclothes. He turned round three times and then sat neatly down with his front paws tucked under him.

'Rosemary, you have a great deal to learn, but you have a kind heart and the right sort of hands.'

She was rubbing him under his chin and feeling the soft vibration of the beginnings of a purr. Rosemary stroked him in silence for a few minutes, and then she said:

'If I've got a lot to learn, please don't go to sleep now, but begin teaching me. What shall we do if Mrs Walker says we mayn't keep you?'

'That's neither here nor there. In any case I can't stay, at least, not very long.'

'Can't stay?' said Rosemary in dismay. 'But why? You're mine! I bought you with my own money!'

'For which, believe me, I shall be always grateful. But you are only fulfilling the prophecy.'

'What prophecy? Oh, do explain!' said Rosie, bouncing with impatience so that the bed creaked. 'I don't know what you are talking about!'

'I said you had a lot to learn,' said Carbonel coolly. 'Sit still and I will try to explain. In the first place you thought you had bought a common witch's cat. Mind you, I'm not blaming you. A very natural mistake. You were not to know that I am a Royal Cat.'

'Gracious!' said Rosemary in a voice that squeaked with excitement. 'But how did you ...?'

'Don't interrupt,' said Carbonel, 'I'm telling you. I was stolen from my cradle when I was a mere kitten. There was a prophecy among my people that something like that would happen one day. SHE stole me. Always ambitious, she was, and nothing would satisfy her but a Royal Cat to run her errands and sit on her broom. Oh, she was a proud one in those days. Handsome they say she was once, too, though you wouldn't think so now.'

'How horrid of her to steal a kitten!' breathed Rosemary indignantly.

'Yes,' said the cat, gazing out of the window with his great amber eyes, not as if he was looking at the roofs and chimneys, but as though he was seeing something quite different. 'I was so young that my eyes were still blue, and my tail no longer than your little finger. But I knew the Royal Rules. I learnt 'em as soon as my eyes were open. I can just remember my mother, a beautiful, smoke grey Persian she was, saying to me: "My son," she used to say, "my little son, never forget you are a Prince. Behave like one, even if you do not feel like one or look like one." I never forgot her words, so I never lost my self respect. Many's the time when I've been too

26

hungry to sleep I've repeated the Rules over and over to myself, till at last I dropped off.'

'Poor little kitten!' said Rosemary softly.

'But it had its moments,' he went on. 'I took to the broomstick business like a duck to water. Oh, those were the days, when you raced together through the tumbling sky, with the Milky Way crackling below, and the wind in your fur strong enough to tear the whiskers off you! Or leaping and plunging through the midnight sky with a host of others, and the earth twirling beneath you no bigger than a bobbin!'

He was standing now with his back arched and bristling, making strange cat noises in his throat. It was growing dusk, and his eyes glowed hotly. Rosemary waited, a little awed, till the noises in his throat subsided, and then she put out a timid hand and stroked the bristling fur. The cat started and came to himself again. She stroked him gently till the only sign of his excitement was in the twitching end of his tail.

'But why did you not run away?' asked Rosemary presently.

'Because the magic was too strong for me. There was nothing for it but to wait until the prophecy was fulfilled. It went like this ...

> *A kit among the stars shall sit*
> *Beyond the aid of feline wit.*
> *Empty Royal throne and mat,*
> *Till Three Queens save a princely cat.*

'And did you sit among the stars?' asked Rosie.

'Of course,' said Carbonel, 'many a night. On Christian name terms with some of them I was ... But don't go and start me off again.'

'I'm beginning to see!' said Rosemary, bouncing up

27

and down again. 'My Queen Victoria farthings are the Three Queens, and they bought you from ... from the old woman.'

'You'd better call her Mrs Cantrip. That's the name she goes by.'

'And now you are free! Oh, Carbonel! How lovely. I'm so glad.' But Carbonel did not seem to share her excitement.

'That's not all,' he said soberly. 'The prophecy is fulfilled and I am free from HER. I did try to escape, I was a kitten of spirit, but of course she caught me. As a punishment, and to make quite certain, she put another spell on me, and until that is broken I must be your slave instead. It was sheer extravagance throwing good magic about like that, but just like her. Spiteful.'

'But I don't want a slave! Carbonel dear, how can we undo it?'

'I don't know,' said the black cat soberly. 'That's just it. It was a Silent Magic – they're the worst kind – and of course as it was silent I didn't hear it. All I do know is that it must be undone with all the same things with which it was made. If you want to undo it you must have the hat and the cauldron. The broom you have already.'

'But, of course, I want to undo the spell and set you free! Didn't you see what she did with the other things?'

'SHE sold them when I was away on an errand so that I should not know where they are. When we find them we've still got to discover the Silent Magic.' There was silence in the little room, which was almost dark now. Even the noise of her mother's sewing machine had stopped. Rosemary put her arm comfortingly round Carbonel.

'We're jolly well going to find everything. The first

thing to do is to discover what has happened to the hat and the cauldron. We will start immediately after breakfast tomorrow!'

Suddenly she realized how sleepy she was. 'We'd better go to bed now.' She padded across the linoleum of the bedroom floor and put the broom in the wardrobe. Before she slipped between the sheets she put both arms round Carbonel and gave him a hug, a thing she would have been rather shy of doing when she could hear him talking. But Carbonel seemed to bear her no malice and gave her cheek a little lick. Rosemary lay down and tucked up her linoleum-chilled toes in her nightdress. She was just dropping off to sleep when she thought to herself, 'He didn't tell me who his people are, or where they live.'

She was just wondering whether to get out of bed to fetch the broom to ask him, when somehow it was morning. The sun was streaming through the window and her mother was knocking on the door.

4

The summoning words

THE first thing that Rosemary thought of when she woke was Carbonel. She sat up and called him softly, but there was no answer. He was not on the bed, or under it. He was not even on the dusty little lead roof outside her window. Thinking back, the whole thing seemed so unbelievable that she began to wonder if perhaps she had dreamed it all. But when she went to look into the wardrobe there was the broom, looking rather forlorn in the corner behind her winter coat. Hearing her wrestling with the wardrobe which had a habit of sticking, Mrs Brown called through the door:

'Rosie! Get dressed, darling. Breakfast is nearly ready and I don't want to be late on my first day.' So Rosemary hurried.

Although they could use Mrs Walker's kitchen with the big black cooker, there was a gas ring and a fire in their room which they used whenever it was possible. With miracles of timing they managed to cook most of their meals here. Rosemary made the toast while her mother tidied the bedrooms.

'I meant to go and ask Mrs Walker about your Pussums before I went this morning,' called Mrs Brown through the open door, 'but I doubt if I shall have time.'

'He isn't here, Mummy. When I woke up this morning he had gone. But I am quite sure he will come back. And please don't call him Pussums, he doesn't like it. His name is Carbonel.' Her mother laughed again.

'What a grand name! You know, if you brush him and feed him up I think he will be a beautiful cat ... If he comes back. I had better wait until this evening, then if he is here I will go and see Mrs Walker. I do hope I can persuade her. It would be such company for you. Rosie, darling, do be careful!'

Through the half-open door drifted the unmistakable smell of burning toast. The idea that Carbonel really might not come back filled Rosemary with such alarm that she forgot what she was doing. But of course he would come back! All the same it was a worrying idea. A second piece of toast was smoking ominously when her mother came in.

'Rosie, how careless of you! Sitting there looking at it burning!'

'I'm sorry, Mummy, I really am. I was thinking how awful it would be if Carbonel didn't come back. I'll eat the scraped bits of toast myself, really I will.'

'Are you sure you won't be lonely while I'm away, darling?' said her mother anxiously over their boiled eggs.

'Not a bit!' said Rosemary, with such conviction that her mother was comforted. 'When Carbonel comes back,' Rosemary said to herself, 'we will search the town until we find the hat and the cauldron, and I expect it will take days.'

'I want you to take the dressing-gown round to Miss Withers for me this morning. I finished it last night,' said Mrs Brown. 'You had better go by bus, and be careful to change when you get to the Town Hall.'

To spend the morning going with a parcel to the other end of the town was the last thing that Rosemary wanted to do, but as she could not explain why, there was no help for it.

After her mother had gone Rosemary tidied the rooms and washed the dishes. Egg, as everyone knows, is one of the most clinging of things to wash away, and it all seemed to take her a very long time. When at last she had finished Carbonel had still not returned. She set out with her parcel, after leaving a saucer of milk in case he came back while she was away. She had half thought of using the broom again, and had got as far as peering into the gloom of the wardrobe, but the faint quiver she felt in the handle, without Carbonel to advise her, was a little alarming, so she said as carelessly as she could, 'I just looked in to see if you were all right,' and shut the door again rather hurriedly.

It took her a long time to find the right house, but when she did Miss Withers gave her a piece of seed cake, which she did not much like, and sixpence, which she did. The sixpence she took to the fishmonger on her way home. He was a large man with large rubber boots and large hands permanently spangled with fish scales. As he was an old friend of Rosemary's she told him what she wanted the fish for. He gave her half-a-pound of Coley and three shrimps, and he would only take four-pence.

'The Coley's for bread, as you might say, and the shrimpses is for jam,' he explained.

Rosemary burst eagerly into the room when she reached home. The saucer she had left on the hearth-rug was empty and polished clean, and Carbonel was lying curled up beside it. Rosemary dashed off for the broom and came whirling back.

THE SUMMONING WORDS

'Carbonel, you are very, very naughty! I've been so worried. Where have you been?'

The black cat stretched himself and yawned so that she could see his magnificent white teeth and his pink tongue, frilled like a flower petal, between.

'I don't know what you are making a fuss about,' he said. 'You could have said the Words and called me back again any time you wanted to.'

'What Words?' said Rosemary.

'Oh, didn't I tell you.' She shook her head. 'The Summoning Words. You simply say ...

> *By squeak of bat,*
> *And brown owl's hoot,*
> *By hellebore,*
> *And mandrake root*
> *Come swift, and silent*
> *As the tomb,*
> *Dark minion*
> *Of the twiggy broom.*

'The merest doggerel I know, but it works. It wouldn't be so humiliating if it were better poetry,' he said bitterly. 'Whenever you say it I'm bound to come, no matter how important the business I may be engaged upon. Have you never seen a black cat hurrying relentlessly along as though he's being pulled by an invisible string? Well, that is what has happened to him, not a doubt.'

Rosie repeated the rhyme until she had learned it by heart.

'It doesn't sound very polite,' she said doubtfully, 'I wouldn't quite like to call you, "minion of the twiggy broom".'

'Well, you'll have to get over that if you want to

33

summon me. You can't expect magic to be lady-like. And that reminds me. I was looking at the broom before you came in and there is precious little life in the old thing.'

Rosemary looked at it thoughtfully. It was indeed a sad sight. It reminded her of a parrot she had once seen that was moulting.

'When the last of those twigs drop off, her power has gone, and it will be too late to find the cauldron and the steeple hat, and I shall be your slave for ever whether you want it or not.'

'Couldn't we mend it somehow?' said Rosemary. 'I could tie on the twigs with string or raffia or something.' Carbonel was horrified.

'Good gracious, no! You can't mend magic with string!' he said in a shocked voice. 'You will be suggesting glue and tin-tacks next. A few weeks ago the cauldron sprang a leak, and SHE insisted on filling up the hole with one of those pot-mender things you get at an ironmonger's, at sixpence a card. And what was the result?' He paused dramatically.

'What?' breathed Rosemary.

'Her spells worked out lumpy. But I tell you what, we've no time to lose. We'd better start searching this afternoon.'

They had their dinner first. Rosie cooked the fish on the gas ring, and then she warmed up the stew that her mother had left her. They ate together in companionable silence on the hearth-rug. Carbonel seemed really touched by the three shrimps.

'A Prince of the Royal Blood,' he said with emotion, 'and yet nobody before has given me shrimps. I shall not forget.'

When they had finished they decided on the plan of

action. It was agreed that they would do best to go back
to Fairfax Market.

'We must take the broom with us so that I can talk to
you, but we mustn't ride on it. I've still got tuppence
from this morning so we can take a bus there, but we
shall have to walk home.'

5

The search begins

THEY reached the market without any adventures.
The bus conductor was quite nice about Carbonel going
on top, and insisted on calling Rosemary 'Miss Whit-
tington', which made everyone in the bus laugh.
When they reached the Market it was looking as she
had expected to find it the day before. There was a
jolly bustle of busy people with bulging shopping bags
and baskets, with the noise of people chatting, and
stallholders crying their wares. Rosemary could
have happily spent the afternoon just looking round,
but she knew that more serious work was on hand.
They had agreed to go round all the stalls that sold
second-hand things first, in the hope that Mrs Cantrip
might have sold the hat or the cauldron to one of
them, and all the time they were to keep a look-out
for the old woman herself. There was always the chance
that they might find her there. Rather regretfully
Rosemary left the cheerful stalls that sold fruit and
groceries, and cotton frocks, and china ornaments.
The second-hand stalls were on the edge of the Market,
near the spot where Rosemary had bumped into Mrs
Cantrip.

They were a little forlorn, these stalls, like the people
who kept them. There were ricketty bedsteads and
lumpy mattresses for sale, chipped chests of drawers, and
piles of old shoes and gramophone records, and bundles
of spoons and forks tied up like bunches of flowers.
There was an old-fashioned hip bath full of oddments

marked 'All in this lot sixpence' which Rosemary would have liked to explore.

'Isn't it funny how old clothes seem to go on being like the people who have worn them,' she said to Carbonel, looking at a limp hat with feathers on it that was perched jauntily on top of a large chipped china jug.

'That is just what I say,' said an old man who was sitting on a chair behind a trestle table covered with old books. Seeing no one else near, he thought she was addressing him.

'There's more profit on new 'uns, but not the interest, I always say. Was you wanting something, dearie?'

He looked a kindly little man, and Rosemary plucked up enough courage to say, 'Please, have you got such a thing as a witch's hat?' The old man began to laugh, and he laughed until the laugh turned into a wheezy cough. When he had recovered, he wiped his red-rimmed eyes and said, 'No, dearie, nor no fairy wands, neither. They're in short supply at present.' And he went off into another wheezy laugh at his own joke.

Rosemary moved on to the next stall. Quite clearly, she decided, she must use more guile.

'Why don't you use your eyes more!' said Carbonel crossly. 'That's the worst of humans. They will talk too much.'

But use her eyes as she would, Rosemary could see no trace of the hat or the cauldron. There were half-a-dozen possible stalls, but she looked and looked and hung about until she felt she could write down from memory exactly what was for sale on each one. So she decided to walk round the Market on the chance of seeing Mrs Cantrip again. She walked all the way round, which took some time because she could not help stopping to look at most of the stalls, and then she found herself back at the wheezy old man. All this time Carbonel had padded quietly after her. Her legs were aching by now, so she sat down on an empty packing-case, and because she felt it was too public to talk to Carbonel she just stroked him instead. Suddenly the wheezy old man said:

'Like an apple, ducks?'

It was rather a hard, green apple, but Rosemary was very grateful for it. She thanked him gravely and munched away.

'That your cat?' asked the old man. Rosemary nodded. 'I don't know when I see such a big 'un, except it was one I saw yesterday on this very spot. Belonged to an old woman. She was a caution!' He broke off to laugh wheezily again.

'You see some queer things in my trade, but I never see'd a queerer than she was. Like an old rag bag, with a little hat on top smart as kiss yer 'and. What's the matter, ducks, a bit of apple gone down the wrong way?'

Rosemary nodded and wiped her eyes.

'Was she selling anything?' she asked as carelessly as she could when she had stopped coughing.

The old man wheezed again, but this time with indignation.

'She stands next to me, and all she's got to sell are an old hat – you never saw such a wreck of an old thing, black it was, with a point – and an old coal-scuttle, one of them with three feet and a handle over the top. Fair crocked with soot, it was.'

'How queer,' said Rosemary. 'Did she sell them?'

The old man went off into such a prolonged wheeze that she could have shaken him with impatience. When at last he emerged he said, 'Ah, she sold 'em right enough. There'd me been 'ere since nine o'clock, and all I'd sold was a book of sermons marked down to tuppence, and a pair of button boots, and 'ere is this old besom setting up for 'alf an hour, and blessed if she don't sell 'er 'at and 'er coal-scuttle right off! Some people don't reckernize 'igh class goods when they sees 'em. Ah, and where was 'er licence I should like to know?' he added darkly, dusting a glass case full of moth-eaten birds as he spoke.

'But what sort of people bought them?' asked Rosemary, quite surprised at her own cunning.

'Well, I didn't see who bought the coal-scuttle. I'm not a one to go Nosey Parkering. But business being slack, I noticed a youngish fellow bargain with 'er for the 'at. Something artistic I'd say by the look on 'im. You gets to be a student of 'uman nature in my job. First thing I sizes up their clothes. 'Is was good but wore. Fifteen bob I'd 'ave given for 'is coat, and a tanner for 'is 'at, not a penny more, but a gentleman, mind. And would you believe it, when she asked a pound for her old 'at, 'e didn't beat 'er down more than a couple of bob. Eighteen shillings 'e paid 'er for it, and looked at it all the time as if it was a picture of 'is long lost ma. "Most interesting," 'e kept saying, "A genuine seventeenth century beaver wotsit." And the old woman grinning and cackling like a lunatic.'

'Who ever could it have been?' said Rosemary.

'Well, that's what I says to myself. A chap wot's silly enough to cough up the best part of a quid for something the cat might 'ave brought in, is too good to lose sight on. So I says wouldn't 'e like to 'ave a look at some of my 'ats? But, bless you, 'e wouldn't even look at my Leghorn with the roses. But when 'e'd gone I did find an

'Did it tell you his name?' asked Rosemary.

old envelope. Dropped it, as like as not, when 'e got out
'is note-case.'

'Did it tell you his name?' asked Rosemary, hardly
able to hide her eagerness.

'No! Just my luck. It only said "To the Occupier",
and 'is address underneath. It was one of those pow-
dered soap coupons to buy a monster packet of Lathero
for the price of a little 'un. I've got it somewhere.' The
old man rummaged about in his many pockets.

' 'Ere it is. The Occupier. You can 'ave it if you like.
I daresay it would come in handy for your ma. My old
woman don't hold with these new fangled things.'

'Oh, thank you!' said Rosemary, and there was no
doubt she meant it. She skipped off, clutching the envelope, and sat down on an upturned bucket behind a
battered wardrobe where she was unlikely to be over-
heard talking to Carbonel. 'It says "*To the Occupier, 101
Cranshaw Road, Netherley*".'

'You really handled that quite creditably,' said
Carbonel.

'I wished we could go there straight away, but it is
four o'clock already, and I promised I would have tea
ready for Mummy when she came home. We had better
go.' Rosemary jumped up and started to walk rapidly
the way they had skimmed so easily the day before on
the broom-stick. But with the letter in her pocket, the
feeling that they had achieved something made the way
home seem quite short. Carbonel padded silently on in
front.

6

Mrs Walker says 'no'

MRS BROWN arrived just as Rosemary had finished laying tea. The kettle was boiling, and they sat down to a companionable meal of buttered toast and strawberry jam, with a large saucer of milk for Carbonel.

'I hope it wasn't too dull all by yourself, dear,' said her mother anxiously.

'Oh, no, Mummy, Carbonel and I went for a walk after we had had our dinner and it was ... most interesting.' Her mother smiled.

'Well, I've got a surprise for you. You know how you have always wanted to see Mrs Pendlebury Parker's house? Well, tomorrow she wants you to go with me and spend the day.'

'Goodness!' said Rosemary. 'How lovely.'

And then she remembered how she had meant to spend the next day looking for Cranshaw Road.

'But shouldn't I be in the way?' she said uncertainly.

'Good gracious, not a bit in a house that size! You see, Mrs Pendlebury Parker has a young nephew coming to stay with her, and as she doesn't know any children she asked if you would come and play with him. He is just about your age.'

Now in any other circumstances Rosemary would have been delighted at the very idea of seeing for herself the glories of Tussocks, which sounded from her mother's description like a fairy tale palace. It never occurred to Mrs Brown that there could be anything that her young daughter would rather do next day, so that she did not notice Rosemary's lack of enthusiasm.

'You had better wear your new gingham frock. It is lucky it is clean. Now as soon as we've cleared away I'll go down and ask Mrs Walker if we may keep the cat. He is a handsome animal. I do hope she will say "yes".'

'I'll wash up the tea things, Mummy, if you will go and ask her now,' said Rosemary.

Mrs Brown went down the six flights of stairs and Rosemary folded up the cloth and got out the enamel bowl for washing up. It took rather a long time to clear away as she was only using one hand. The other was holding the broom so that she could talk to Carbonel.

'If only I could have gone to Tussocks another day!' she complained. Carbonel seemed unruffled.

'As long as you don't use the broom and go wearing it out for nothing, there is no need to get into such a fantod about it. If you are going to do magic, even elementary stuff, you'll have to learn that time is merely a figure of speech.'

'Is it?' said Rosemary. Half her attention was concentrated on the wobbly pile of cups and saucers she was carrying with one hand, and at the same time she was wondering if she could tell Miss Pettigrue that time was merely a figure of speech next time she was late for school.

'Besides,' went on Carbonel, 'I have important things to see to that would not interest you.'

'How do you know they would not interest me?' said Rosemary, a little ruffled. It really was difficult to clear away with one hand. 'Oh, don't go to sleep, Carbonel! Mummy will be back at any minute, and then you won't be able to talk to me any more.'

43

The cat, who had curled himself up on the hearth-rug, yawned elaborately. 'Well, you were not interested enough to ask me what I was doing last night and this morning,' he said huffily. 'Not so much as a "Hope you enjoyed yourself".' He turned in his paws and closed his eyes to mere golden slits. 'Besides,' he added sleepily, 'you really can't wash-up with one hand, so you had better put the broom down,' and he shut his eyes firmly. Not another word would he say.

Rosemary splashed the plates so vigorously that a good deal of the water slopped over on to the floor, which made her cross. 'Really, Carbonel behaves sometimes as though he has bought me, not the other way round.'

But Rosemary was not a sulky child, and as soon as she heard her mother coming slowly across the landing she forgot everything except the fact that they sounded like the footsteps of someone who has not good news to tell.

'It's no use, Rosie,' said Mrs Brown sadly, 'Mrs Walker won't hear of having a cat in the house!'

'Mummy, what shall we do?'

'Poppet, I said everything I could think of to make her change her mind. I told her how useful he would be for catching mice. But she only sniffed and said there had never been a mouse in the house in her day. I'm so sorry, darling. I'm afraid he will have to go.'

'But I can't send him away, not now I can't!' said Rosemary, scooping Carbonel up and hugging him fiercely. 'Darling Carbonel, how could I?' Two fat tears went rolling down her cheeks and fell with a splash on to the cat's black fur. He struggled violently, and when Rosemary put him down he stalked off, shaking each paw in turn.

44

'If only we had our own little house, you should have half-a-dozen cats,' said Mrs Brown.

'I don't want half-a-dozen cats. I want Carbonel.'

'Well, use my hankie and cheer up. Suppose we keep him until the morning and see if we can think of something. I never thought I should ever want to live in a house that was full of mice!' said Mrs Brown. Rosemary was startled to hear Carbonel say 'Don't worry, you will!'

She looked up in alarm, but her mother was quietly putting the china away in the cupboard. Then she noticed that when she had flung herself down to pick up Carbonel she had put her hand accidentally on the handle of the broom which was sticking out from where she had pushed it under the sofa. Of course, her mother could not have heard. Rosemary looked sharply at Carbonel, but he was sitting on the hearth-rug, absorbed in washing himself, with one of his hind legs sticking straight up in the air.

'Will you come and talk to me in bed like you did last night?' she whispered. Carbonel paused for a moment.

'Not tonight. I shall be too busy.'

'And please don't be cross with me,' she bent down to whisper, 'it isn't fair.'

But her mother had returned and Carbonel did not reply. Instead he lifted his head and with a warm, wet, rasping tongue gave her cheek a little lick. Comforted, Rosemary sat beside him on the hearth-rug and stroked him very gently on the top of his satin-smooth head.

7

Carbonel and Mrs Walker

WHEN Rosemary woke next morning it was not to a feeling of pleasure at the prospect of the visit to Tussocks, but to one of uneasiness. At first she could not think what it was that was worrying her, but as her mind wandered sleepily back over the events of yesterday, it came to her quite suddenly. Mrs Walker would not let her keep Carbonel. And as suddenly she was wide awake and jumping out of bed.

The cat was not in her bedroom. Neither was he in the sitting room, where her mother was getting breakfast.

'Never mind!' said Mrs Brown when she saw her daughter's anxious face. 'Perhaps it is just as well he should take himself off, if Mrs Walker won't let us keep him. I have been wondering how on earth we could find another home for him. But go and get dressed, darling. Had you forgotten you are coming with me today?'

Rosemary put on her newest gingham frock with none of the satisfaction that it usually gave her. She tidied her bedroom and made her bed with special care, and all the time she was making desperate plans for keeping Carbonel secretly in the tumbledown rabbit hutch in the yard.

'But I don't suppose he'd so much as look at a rabbit hutch,' she thought, as she smoothed the bedspread with the exactness of thoughtful misery. 'He would probably be offended at the very idea.'

During a rather silent breakfast, Rosemary was making patterns on her buttered toast with the point of her knife when there was an unmistakable 'Mew' outside the door. Rosemary ran to open it, and sure enough, there was Carbonel! He trotted into the room with a smug expression on his face, without so much as a glance at Rosemary. Her mother, who was secretly feeling that it would have been much simpler if the cat had not come back, looked at her daughter's worried face and reproached herself.

'Let's give him some milk, Poppet. But what to do about him I just don't know! We simply must get ready to go now.'

Rosemary had such a tight feeling in her throat that she did not dare to say anything. She poured out a saucer of milk and was listening to the cat's rhythmical lap-lap, lap-lap, when there was a knock on the door. Before her mother had time to say 'Come in!' Mrs Walker burst into the room.

'Oh, Mrs Brown!' she said. 'It's a judgement on me for saying you could not keep your cat. I never saw the like!'

'Good gracious, what has happened? You look so upset! Now do sit down and let me give you a cup of tea. It has not been standing long.'

'The kitchen!' gasped Mrs Walker. 'It's full of mice, hundreds of them! You never saw anything like it! And me that's always said that mice is vermin, and there's only vermin where there's dirt, and not a mouse in the house in all the fifteen years I've been here. Would you believe it? I opened the kitchen door to cook my old man a pair of kippers for 'is breakfast – he's partial to kippers, Alfred is – and it fair turned me over. I can't abide them!'

Rosemary, who gathered it was mice that Mrs Walker could not abide, and not kippers, looked at Carbonel. He was tactfully keeping out of sight behind the horse-hair sofa, but she could see that he had finished the saucer of milk and was looking as self-satisfied as if it had been a bowl of cream. He opened his great golden eyes and looked full at Rosemary, and could it be? She was not quite certain, but it almost seemed as if one eye flickered in a wink.

'I shall never feel easy in that kitchen again,' said Mrs Walker.

'But it will be quite all right,' said Rosemary. 'You see, we did not get rid of my cat last night.'

'We were going to see if we could find a home for him today,' broke in Mrs Brown hurriedly.

Rosemary picked up Carbonel; it needed both arms. 'But isn't it a good thing we've still got him? Because I'm sure he will get rid of your mice for you.'

'I think you would find the very fact that there was a cat in the house would keep the mice away,' said Mrs Brown.

'Well, he's a handsome animal, that I will say,' said Mrs Walker. 'You can keep him and welcome, if only he'll get rid of the mice!'

'Rosie, dear, take him down to the kitchen and leave him there ...'

'Yes, dearie, do! And I'll give your Mum a hand with her dirty crocks; I expect she wants to be getting off to work. I couldn't stay in the kitchen while ...' Mrs Walker broke off and shuddered.

Carbonel had already struggled out of Rosemary's arms and was standing expectantly by the door. As her mother said, he might have understood every word. She opened the door and he ran down the stairs so quickly that Rosemary had no time to fetch the broom-stick. So it was an entirely one-sided conversation she held with him on the way down. Explanations would have to wait till later.

'I don't know how you did it, but it was very clever of you! And now you can stay with us for always and always! At least, until you have to go away. How glorious!'

They had reached the basement by now, where Mrs Walker lived with her husband. Carbonel was scratching impatiently at the kitchen door. Rosemary turned the handle and looked in. The noise of squeaking was deafening. There were mice all over the place; they were scuttering over the linoleum and running up and down the lace curtains that hid the dismal view of the dust-bins in the yard. They were playing hide-and-seek in the rag rug on the hearth and nibbling the loaf that stood on the table. There was even one peering out of the Coronation mug that held the place of honour on the mantelpiece. Rosemary took all this in in a flash, and at the very same time she remembered something which in the excitement of the moment she had forgotten. She remembered the way in which cats generally get rid of mice. Surely Carbonel was not going to eat them? She shut the door hurriedly and retreated to the bottom step of the flight of stairs with her eyes tight shut and her fingers in her ears. Of course it was silly to expect a cat not to behave like a cat, even if he was a prince. 'All the same,' thought Rosemary, 'there must have been hundreds of them! It seems horrible, because he must have tricked them somehow into coming, and the one in the Coronation mug did look so sweet!'

It seemed hours before she plucked up enough courage to open her eyes and take her fingers from her ears.

but really it was only a few minutes. There was complete silence; not a squeak was to be heard. Then from the other side of the door came a faint 'Mew'. She stood up and walked slowly to the door. Once they had had a cat who caught a mouse now and then. He would eat up every bit except the tail, and that he would present to her mother as a great prize. Would she find ...? But wondering only made it worse. She took a deep breath and flung open the door. There was no sign of any movement, not a mouse was to be seen, but where the loaf of bread had been on the trencher were now only a few crumbs. Carbonel stalked past her slowly and with great dignity. Licking his whiskers he mounted the stairs as though it was rather an effort.

Mrs Walker was waiting for them.

'You 'ave been quick, dearie! Has 'e done it?'

Rosemary nodded.

'Thank you ever so! Well, it beats me how it happened. Not a mouse in fifteen years and then 'undreds!'

'I have heard of mice moving in a body from some building which has been pulled down,' said Mrs Brown.

'Depend upon it, that's it!' said Mrs Walker. 'Though why they have to pick on my house to come to I really do not see!'

'It certainly is a most extraordinary thing,' said Mrs Brown.

'Oh well, I'll be glad to have a cat around, Rosie, so I'll feed 'im while you are gone. I 'ear you are going with your Ma today. Well, I must get on with my old man's kippers.' And full of smiles Mrs Walker went downstairs.

'It's very odd,' said Mrs Brown when she had gone, 'but it could not have happened at a better time for us! Just look at that cat!'

Carbonel was lying on the hearth-rug, looking so portly that it was not surprising that he seemed reluctant to curl up in his usual way. Rosemary wondered if perhaps he could not curl up if he wanted to. He lay stretched on his side, purring deeply.

'You had better go and get ready,' said Mrs Brown. 'Put on your better sandals, the ones that have just been mended, and don't forget a clean hankie.'

When Rosemary was holding the broom-stick and could hear him talk she was always a little in awe of Carbonel, but now he was silent and sleeping like any hearth-rug animal, so without any ceremony she scooped him up in her arms, too sleepy to struggle, and dropped him on her bed. Then she whirled to the wardrobe and fetched the broom.

'How could you!' she said, stamping her foot. 'It was hateful of you!' Carbonel opened his eyes sleepily, and his purr took on a deeper, slower note.

'I've never had such a meal in my life,' he said dreamily.

'Did you eat them all?' said Rosemary incredulously.

'Heads, tails, and backbones,' said Carbonel, 'and left not a wrack behind! Shakespeare,' he added graciously.

'Then I think you ought to be ashamed of yourself! Just for your own ends to eat all those dozens of poor little mice!'

Carbonel opened his eyes very wide.

'Who said anything about mice? It was the kippers I ate, two pairs of them. They were on the floor, and everyone knows that is where the cat's food is put. If they weren't put there on purpose I can't help that. In any case it was the least she could do, putting me to all that trouble. I had to round up all the mice in

Tottenham Grove and then explain what I wanted them to do. It took me all night. I didn't touch a whisker of them,' he said with righteous indignation. 'I'd given them my word, hadn't I? The only way I could get them to come was by promising a truce for six weeks. Oh, they drove a hard bargain, I can tell you. Six weeks without a mouse! It's positive cruelty. Now run away and leave me to sleep it off.' And he curled himself up like a foot-warmer.

Rosemary was filled with a wave of self-reproach. How could she have thought so badly of him? She bent down over the sleeping animal and whispered, 'I'm sorry I was so silly. Please forgive me.'

But there was no answer, so she put the broom in the wardrobe and tip-toed away.

8

Tussocks

BY the time that Rosemary had arrived at Tussocks, Mrs Pendlebury Parker's house, she had decided that she was not going to think about witches, or broomsticks, or anything magic at all for the whole day. It was really rather a relief. She wondered if the house would be anything like she had imagined it, and what the boy she would have to play with would be like.

The house turned out to be larger even than Rosemary had imagined. It had been built in the reign of Queen Victoria, so her mother said, by Mrs Pendlebury Parker's grandfather, who had made a lot of money in cotton, and then moved to the south to try to forget how he had made it. The house had towers with blue slate roofs and battlements of stone and very bright red terra cotta gargoyles all over the place. Although Mrs Brown said it was ugly, Rosemary thought it was beautiful, and would be a wonderful place to play in. They went to a side door where a cheerful-looking maid in a pink striped dress let them in.

'You're to come straight upstairs, Mrs Brown,' she said. 'Mrs P's not up yet. And is this your little girl? Well, if she can keep that young limb out of mischief we shall all be grateful. But when a child is all by himself with nothing to do, it stands to reason there is nothing to do but be naughty.'

Rosemary was far too busy looking about her to listen to the conversation. They walked along several stone-paved passages, up some linoleum-covered stairs, and through a baize door. Here there was no stone or linoleum, but deep red carpet, and the sort of pictures on the walls that Rosemary had only seen in museums. She would like to have stopped to look at them, but she was afraid of being left behind. Presently the maid knocked at one of the doors and when a voice called 'Come in!' she opened it.

'Mrs Brown and the little girl, madam,' she said.

Rosemary was aware of a very large room with a pale blue carpet and great furry white rugs. In a large four-post bed with an immense blue eiderdown, leaning against a great many pillows, sat a plump woman in a very frilly pink bed-jacket. They walked up to the foot of the bed and Rosemary noticed that the lady was not as young as she had thought at first.

'So this is Rosemary!' said Mrs Pendlebury Parker. 'Come here, child.' Rosemary went forward, tripping over a pair of slippers that seemed to consist largely of heels and feathers.

'How do you do?' she said politely.

'Not very well this morning ... My head, you know. But you look a nice little thing. I knew that your good mother could only have a nice little girl, so I thought it would be quite safe to ask you to play with Lancelot. Lance, dear, come here!'

There was a movement behind the heavy, blue damask curtains and a boy about the same height as Rosemary came towards them from the wide window-seat. He was scowling hideously, and his hands were pushed down to the bottom of his pockets.

'Now you two are the same age, so you are sure to be friends!' said Mrs Pendlebury Parker.

The boy scowled more deeply than ever. It was funny, thought Rosemary. Grown-ups took it for granted that children of the same age must always be friends. She found herself thinking that Mrs Pendlebury Parker and Mrs Walker must be about the same age, and yet it was very unlikely that they would be friends.

'Now run along and play, dears, and do try to be good children!'

The boy looked at Rosemary, and with a nod of his head motioned her to the door and followed her out.

When he got outside he blew out his cheeks as though he was a balloon letting itself down.

'She knows I hate it, and she will go on doing it.'

'Who does what?' asked Rosemary.

'Aunt Amabel will call me Lancelot. Just because that was what her father was called – my grandfather, you know – I was called after him, to try to make him forgive Mum. But it didn't, and so I'm branded with an awful name like that for the rest of my life for nothing.'

'What had your mother done?' asked Rosemary with interest.

'Married my father. He was a poor artist. He still is. Daddy says nearly all good artists are poor until they're dead. And now I've got to play with you.'

'Well, I didn't ask to play with you!' said Rosemary. 'Besides, it isn't my fault what your aunt calls you, so I don't see why you should be cross with me.'

The boy looked at her for the first time, and the scowl relaxed. 'I suppose it isn't your fault. I say, you don't look half so bad as I expected. You can call me John – that's my other name. Nobody knows about Lancelot at school. Come on! Let's go into the garden.'

They ran off together through the baize door, down the linoleum-covered stairs, and out into the garden.

'Race you to the end of the terrace!' said John.

They raced, but it was Rosemary who got there first.

There was a semi-circular stone seat at the end with a canopy of pale golden roses growing over it, so they sat down to get their breath back again.

'You know,' said John, 'I thought that any girl that Aunt Amabel produced would be all frills and white shoes, not sandals and a cotton frock like my sister. She's got measles. My sister, I mean. That's why I'm here. She had to go and get it the very day before I came home from school.'

'How sickening for her!'

'Sickening for her?' said John indignantly. 'She's got all the fun of having spots, and cut-out things in bed, and I've only got Aunt Amabel and this ghastly place!'

Rosemary's eyes grew round.

'But this is a lovely house!'

'It would be all right, I suppose, if I was left alone, but it's "Lance, dear, don't do that!" and "Lance, dear, do do the other," and "Keep your feet off the paint," and "Don't touch!" The only decent place is the kitchen garden, and that is pretty good. Let's go and find some goosegogs.'

9

John

THEY spent a happy half-hour among the gooseberry
bushes, where the fruit hung like golden lanterns among
the dark leaves. They ate until the prospect of bursting
even one more on her tongue made Rosemary look at
them with distaste. Then they played Cowboys and Indians, and then they tried trawling along the widest
gravel path with one of the nets off the gooseberry
bushes. But they caught nothing except a couple of
man-eating sharks (they were really sticks), so they
thought they had better put the nets back before any
more holes got torn. Then, feeling rather hot, they came
out of the kitchen garden and lay flat on the dusty grass
under the cedar tree on the lawn. It was really a very
hot day. They could see the main drive from here before
it curved round to the front door. Presently a sleek,
black car slipped down the drive on the way to the
main road.

'How lovely to have a car like that,' said Rosemary,
sitting up and pouring a handful of dust from one
cupped palm to the other.

'Pooh! That's nothing,' said John carelessly. 'Aunt
Amabel has got three, counting the little grey one.'

'Good gracious!' said Rosemary, deeply impressed.
'Have you got three?'

'As a matter of fact we've got four, and a pony,
and ... and an aeroplane. What have you got?'

Rosemary was surprised. Somehow John did not look
like the kind of boy to have a pony or an aeroplane.

There was a darn in the seat of his grey flannel shorts, and the rubber was beginning to peel from the toes of his sandals. She did not boast herself as a rule, but it seemed hard not to be able to produce anything at such a challenge, so without bothering about the consequences she said, 'I've got a witch's broom and a cat that talks.'

'That's silly,' said John. 'You couldn't have.'

Rosemary sat up cross-legged and very strait. Her face had gone quite red.

'I have, so there!'

John rolled over and looked at her.

'All right, you needn't get so waxy!'

'But you don't believe me, and it's true!'

'Bet you can't prove it!'

'Right,' said Rosemary hotly, 'I will! I know a magic spell that will make the cat come to me, whether he wants to or not.'

'All right!' said John, grinning hatefully. 'Say it!'

Rosemary stood up. Could she remember the Summoning Words? She screwed up her eyes and said a little uncertainly:

By squeak of bat
And brown owl's hoot,
By hellebore,
And mandrake root,
Come swift and silent
As the tomb,
Dark minion
Of the twiggy broom.

She opened her eyes again and looked anxiously round. There was no Carbonel.

'I say, you do do it well!' said John with a note of

real admiration in his voice, which at any other time would have given her great satisfaction. But the way in which he did not even trouble to show that he did not believe her, made her bite her lip with vexation. She looked round desperately for Carbonel once more, and seeing nothing but the sun-baked lawn, to her own surprise burst into tears. John sat up.

'I say,' he said awkwardly, 'whatever is the matter? I didn't really think you would believe any of that stuff about me having a pony, and an aeroplane. Of course we haven't. We've only an old rattle-trap of a car. It was only a game. You had better have my hankie. I've got one today,' he said with modest pride. Rosemary was feeling for hers in her knicker leg without success.

'But it is true,' she sniffed obstinately. 'I have got a broom-stick that flies, and a witch's cat ...' And out came the whole story.

John listened with open mouth. She described how she lived with her mother, and how she had gone to Fairfax Market, and all the strange things that had happened since.

'Gosh!' said John, when she had finished. 'I say, you are lucky! Oh, not the broom business. That's all pretend, though you tell it awfully well. I mean you are lucky getting your own dinner, and cooking it yourself on a gas-ring. It must be wizard!'

Rosemary was just going to say once more that it was not pretend, but she stopped herself. After all, she could hardly blame him for not believing her. A week ago she would not have believed it herself, and there was some consolation in John's genuine envy for the gas-ring dinners. A discreet booming noise came from the house.

'That's the first gong for lunch,' said John. 'We'd better go and wash. Aunt Amabel is fussy.'

As they walked towards the house, he told her that although his mother was Mrs Pendlebury Parker's sister, they were always hard-up, that he had a sister of twelve (the one with measles), and a small brother of four, and they lived in the country. It all sounded very jolly.

10

The spell works

LUNCH promised to be rather an alarming meal at first.
Rosemary knew that her mother had hers on a tray in
the sewing room, but she herself was to join Mrs Pendlebury Parker and John in the great dining room, a huge
room with a floor polished like a mirror, and French
windows opening on to the terrace. There was an alarming number of knives and forks by her plate, but by
watching carefully she managed to use the right ones.
Mrs Pendlebury Parker clearly meant to be kind, even
if she was not very understanding, and by the time they
had started on their pudding, which was a wonderful
concoction of fruit and cream, Rosemary had lost her
shyness.

'What an awful lot of washing up there must be
here,' she said as she helped herself to the dish that was
handed round to her.

Mrs Pendlebury Parker smiled, and then she gave a
little scream.

'Good gracious! What's that by your chair?'

Rosemary looked down, and there beside her, covered
with dust, sitting sedately with his tail curled round his
paws, was Carbonel!

'It is my darling cat!' said Rosemary, falling on her
knees beside him, her pudding forgotten.

John stood up to see and spilled his glass of
water.

'Really, Lance dear, how careless of you! Ring for
Walters and ask her to bring a cloth. But what a clever

'*It is my darling cat!*'

pussy, and what a lucky girl you are to have such a faithful friend.'

Mrs Pendlebury Parker bent down and stroked Carbonel, who had struggled from his young mistress.

'He must have walked miles and miles to find you! The dear, faithful Pussicuddlums! Oh, Walters, bring a cloth, please, and mop up this mess. Oh, and I think you had better bring some food for the cat. NOT in darling Popsey Dinkums' dish, I couldn't bear that. Popsey Dinkums was my beautiful prize pussy, Rosemary. The purest gold and such wonderful eyes, you can't think how I miss him since he disappeared four months ago. But this is a most remarkable cat of yours, quite extraordinary!'

Rosemary agreed. 'Just how extraordinary, you have no idea!' she thought to herself. Had Carbonel really come in answer to the Summoning Words? She could think of no other reason. It was pleasant to see John's face with eyes still like saucers. He clearly thought it was due to the spell. Her triumph would have been complete if the cat had been in the least pleased to see her. As it was, he ignored her completely, and was giving Mrs Pendlebury Parker all his attention while she rubbed him behind the ears, talking to him in a kind of baby language that Rosemary privately thought rather silly.

John was automatically eating his pudding, while his round eyes never left Carbonel.

'I was just wondering what we had better do with him until you go home, dear,' said Mrs Pendlebury Parker. 'I don't think he should be allowed to wander off again.'

'Perhaps he could stay with Mummy,' said Rosemary.

'What a good idea! Now finish up your pudding and then you shall take him along. Lancelot dear, you know where the sewing room is.'

Rosemary would have liked a second helping, but she slipped off her chair and with both arms round Carbonel she set off, with John leading the way with the dish of food. It looked very much like chicken.

The sewing room had once been a school-room. It was cool and pleasant, with two comfortable, battered basket chairs, a big table with a sewing machine and a dressmaker's dummy that looked exactly like Mrs Pendlebury Parker. Mrs Brown was finishing her lunch.

'Mummy!' burst out Rosemary. 'Here's Carbonel! He has come all the way from Tottenham Grove to find me. Isn't he clever? And can he stay with you this afternoon until we go home?'

'Of course he can, dear!' Mrs Brown looked anxious. 'I do hope that Mrs Pendlebury Parker was not annoyed?'

'Oh no, not a bit. She was very kind, and ordered this gorgeous dinner for him. We had a heavenly pudding. It looked like sand pies with frothy stuff on top, only it didn't taste like that, of course. Oh, I forgot. This is John.'

John shook hands.

'Are you sure your aunt was not cross about the cat?'

'Aunt Amabel is potty about cats, so it didn't matter a bit. I say, he is walloping down his dinner!'

'Well, he has certainly earned it. What an extraordinary animal he is. What did you two do this morning?' asked Mrs Brown.

'Played,' said John. 'Do you know, it's the first morning I haven't got into trouble since I've been

64

here? I say, I like having Rosemary. Do you think you could ask me to your house one day?'

Mrs Brown smiled ruefully. 'I'm afraid it isn't a house, only three rooms. Wouldn't you find it rather dull?'

'But I shouldn't!' said John. 'We could cook our own dinner. Rosemary says she often does.'

'Oh, yes!' said Rosemary. 'Do let's! What would you like for dinner?'

'Baked beans and sausages,' said John promptly. 'Mummy, please!'

Mrs Brown laughed. 'If it rested with me I should say yes, but it depends on what your aunt thinks about it.'

'May we ask her, Mummy, please, for tomorrow?'

'If you like, dear. Now off with you. I must get on with these curtains.'

Outside on the sun-warmed stone seat with the canopy of yellow roses, they sat and talked.

'You see, if you would let me I could help you find the hat and the cauldron,' said John. After the first surprise of Carbonel's appearance he seemed to have accepted the whole story, as unquestioningly as you accept the fact that the world is round, when apparently it is so very flat.

'That is a good idea,' said Rosemary. 'We should find them much more quickly with two people's brains, and it would be so much more fun. Do let's go and ask your aunt now!'

'No good – she will be having a rest. We had better wait till tea time.'

So they played games until tea, with periodical visits to Mrs Brown and Carbonel, and after tea, which was raspberries and cream, and the thinnest bread and butter that Rosemary had ever seen, they tried their luck. Mrs Pendlebury Parker frowned. 'I don't think Mrs Brown should have suggested such a thing without consulting me first.'

'But she didn't, Aunt Amabel. It was my idea. Mrs Brown said she did not think you would approve, but that, of course, we could if you said yes. Oh, please!'

'But you two children would be quite alone! I don't think that would be at all suitable.'

'We shouldn't really be alone,' said Rosemary. 'At least not more alone than if we were playing in a room here. You see, there is Mrs Walker in the basement, and Mr and Mrs Tonks on the first floor, and the Smithers on the second, and Miss Tidmarsh just below. And we would promise to be sensible!'

'There are other people in the house, then? That does make a difference, of course. As a matter of fact I have to have lunch with Lady Bermondsey tomorrow, and I was wondering ...'

'And besides,' said John, 'Daddy says that you can't have one-sided hospitality – it isn't democratic.'

'So like him,' said Mrs Parker tartly. 'But all the same, if you don't think Mummy would mind ...?'

'Then I may go? Tomorrow? Oh, thank you, Aunt Amabel!'

'I'll take great care of him,' said Rosemary. 'And thank you for a lovely day!'

Mrs Pendlebury Parker laughed and called to John, who was already half-way out of the door:

'Lancelot, tell Jeffries that he had better take Mrs Brown and Rosemary home at five o'clock in the car. I don't see how they could manage with the cat, otherwise.'

11

Showing off

ROSEMARY and her mother thanked Jeffries, the chauffeur, and got out of the car at number ten, Tottenham Grove. Rosemary rather hoped that one of her friends would see them, but the only person to notice was the boy delivering evening papers, and he only noticed Carbonel in her arms.

He sang out rudely:

> *Does your mother want a rabbit?*
> *Skin her one for ninepence!*

She felt Carbonel stiffen angrily.

'Well, darling, did you enjoy it?' said her mother when they reached their room and she was taking off her hat.

'Mummy, it was lovely! I liked John awfully, and the garden, and the scrumptious pudding. And Mrs Pendlebury Parker was very kind! But you only had rice and stewed fruit. I saw when we came to see you.'

'It was very nice rice pudding,' said Mrs Brown as she ran her fingers through her hair. 'And as for Carbonel ...!'

There was a knock on the door.

'Oh dear, that sounds like Mrs Walker again. Come in!' she called.

'Oh, there you are, dear,' panted the landlady. 'These stairs will be the death of me! I just came up to see if the cat was here. It's a funny thing, I'd just put down a plate for 'im this morning with some nice bits of liver, and 'im purring for it like a steam engine, when 'e suddenly lifts up 'is head and gives a little mew, angry like, and off he goes up the area steps as if the dogs was after 'im! And I 'aven't seen him since. I wouldn't like ...'

'Don't worry, Mrs Walker,' said Mrs Brown. 'A most extraordinary thing! He suddenly turned up at Mrs Pendlebury Parker's house this afternoon. It must be every bit of six miles.'

'Well I never!' said Mrs Walker.

Rosemary looked at Carbonel, but he still ignored her, as he had done all afternoon. She was not feeling very comfortable about her own behaviour over the Summoning Words. Was she right to have used them as she did? But as sometimes happens when we are afraid we are in the wrong she took refuge in being cross. She had been looking forward to a good long talk all day, but when she saw him going off with Mrs Walker without so much as a glance in her direction, she said to herself that she didn't care in the least, and that she would not talk to him if she could, and perhaps that would teach him!

By bedtime she would have given a good deal to have seen him curled up on the eiderdown. She could have said the Summoning Words, but she felt a little shy of using them again, and besides, it seemed wasteful to use magic to fetch him from the basement. Rather like hiring a taxi to go to the corner of the road. She knew he would come back in the end, so there was nothing to do but wait patiently.

When her mother had gone next morning, Rosemary tidied up the flat with special care, and then she hurried off to the shops. She bought a pound of sausages, the thin kind, a large tin of baked beans, two cream buns, two gob-stoppers for dessert, a bunch of cornflowers, and two ounces of sprats as a peace offering for Carbonel. The cornflowers were only twopence because they were just beginning to go white at the edges. She would like to have set it all out on her best doll's tea service, but she was not sure if John would laugh, so she decided not to. She poked her head into the wardrobe to see if the broom was all right and, thinking it must be rather dull for the poor thing, she took it out and laid it carefully on her bed with the precious twigs on the pillow.

At 11 o'clock she was watching for John through the window, but it was a large black car that stopped at the door, not the smaller grey one in which they had come last night. John was already on the way upstairs when she ran down. She could see Mrs Walker on the floor below peering suspiciously after him.

'I say, I am glad you've come! I was afraid something would happen to stop you.'

'It's all right, Aunt Amabel has gone on in the car to a committee. Jeffries is coming about three o'clock to take us both back to Tussocks to tea. It's all arranged. I say, where is the cat and the broom?'

'Carbonel has gone off on his own. He does sometimes, you know. I'm afraid he is cross with me about that spell yesterday. But there is the broom ... oh, please be careful!'

John had picked it up without ceremony, and was examining it with an incredulous expression.

'What a mouldy old thing!' he said cheerfully.

'It's not!' said Rosemary hotly. 'And if it was it would be very unkind to tell it so. You must be very gentle with it.'

'Well, how do I make it take me for a ride?'

'You don't make it. You ask it very politely, in rhyme.'

'Do you mean to say that I've got to make up poetry?' said John in the same voice he would have used if he had been asked to jump over the moon.

'I'll do it, because it is my broom,' said Rosemary. 'At least, I'll try. It must be only a tiny ride because of not wearing out the magic. I should think round the sitting room.'

They fetched a piece of paper, and after much argument and biting of the pencil they produced a rhyme that they both secretly thought rather good.

'Now, stand astride the handle, say it aloud, and then hold tight!'

John did as he was told and said loudly:

> *Round and round the sitting room*
> *Kindly take me, magic broom.*

With a jerk that nearly threw him off, the broom rose into the air with John astride, and swept into the sitting room. Round and round it went, about three feet from the floor. It was not very comfortable, because unless he kept his legs straight out in front they bumped into the furniture. As it was, he knocked the cornflowers over, so that the water streamed over Mrs Brown's best tablecloth that Rosemary had taken without permission. The broom took the corners with a violence that would not have disgraced a Dodg'em. But John held on and went careering round with shining eyes, making penetrating jet plane noises.

Rosemary was delighted. Now he would have to believe that the story she had told him was true! Round and round went the broom. Presently John stopped making jet noises, and a little later he stopped smiling.

'I say, Rosie!' he called, 'I think I've had enough. How do I stop it?'

'Oh, dear!' said Rosemary. 'We didn't say in the rhyme how many times round we wanted it to go.'

'Well, hurry up and tell it now ... I'm not feeling very well.'

'I'll try,' said Rosemary anxiously, 'but I shall have to get some paper. I can't do poetry without.'

She had no idea what they had done with the pencil, and when she found it at last under the bed she was so flustered she could think of no rhymes at all. By this time a very pale John was clinging on to the broom with both arms. Rosemary bit the pencil and screwed up her eyes until it hurt, but it was no use. She could think of no poetry at all. John was just saying faintly:

'I think I'm going ... to be ...' when Carbonel walked silently into the room.

Rosemary fell on her knees beside him.

'Oh, Carbonel, darling! Please, please stop the broom! We forgot to say how many times round it was to go, and now it won't stop! And John looks as if he's dying. Whatever shall we do?'

There was no reply, only a faint moan from John, and Rosemary added:

'But it is no good telling me because I can't hear!'

The cat struggled free from her enclosing arms and stalked into the centre of the room. There was a pause, and then, haltingly, as though he was waiting to be prompted, John said faintly:

Forgive my rude untutored tongue,
Remember I am very young.
On the bed I pray you lay me,
Or my ride will surely slay me!

71

And at once, gently as a boat sailing on a peaceful sea, the broom skimmed the bedroom and settled down on Rosemary's bed, where John lay beside it, thankful for the feel of solid, if rather lumpy, mattress beneath him. Rosemary, wide-eyed and anxious, followed with Carbonel. The black cat put his front paws on the bed and looked at John's closed eyes and pale face, and Rosemary quickly put her hand on the broom.

'He'll be all right in a minute. It all comes of showing off,' said Carbonel severely. 'First it was yesterday, you saying the Summoning Words, and me just settling down to my dinner ... as nice a bit of liver as I've ever seen ... to hurry six miles in the sweltering heat, and for what? Nothing at all,' he added bitterly. 'If you wanted to show what you can do, why couldn't you have done something flashy ... like turning this boy here into a beetle, or something ...'

'No fear!' said John, struggling into a sitting position. The colour was returning to his cheeks.

'Besides, I don't know how to turn people into beetles,' said Rosemary.

'I suppose you don't,' said Carbonel grudgingly. 'But there is no excuse for showing off with the broom, when the poor old thing wants all the rest and quiet she can get. I saw several more twigs on the floor next door. And you must have offended her into the bargain. That's why I put in that bit about "Pardon my untutored tongue." She only takes her corners like that when she is upset.'

'I expect that was me,' said John. 'I called her a ... a mouldy old thing, but I'm awfully sorry. I think it's a simply wizard broom!'

Rosemary felt the broom wince in a bridling sort of way under her hand.

'There you go again! It isn't a wizard broom. Don't you know a witch's broom when you see one?'

Rosemary put out her hand and stroked Carbonel rather shyly on the top of his head with one finger.

'Please don't be cross any more. I said the Summoning Words because I couldn't bear John not to believe about you. I only half thought they would work when I said them, and I promise never to say them again, unless it's really important.'

Carbonel looked a little less severe. Rosemary transferred her stroking finger to the soft part underneath his chin, and he did not seem to mind.

'But it is no good you doing slovenly spells like that,' he said more gently. 'The idea of not saying when you wanted the broom to stop! If I had not come back it would have to have gone on going round and round until all the twigs fell out of its tail, and it might have taken months!'

John shuddered.

'Or until I could think of a rhyme, I suppose,' said Rosemary.

'Which would have been much the same thing, seemingly,' said Carbonel tartly.

12

Carbonel explains

'I SAY,' said John. 'If you want to take care of the twigs on the broom, why don't you wrap something round them – brown paper, or something.'

'It might help,' said the cat doubtfully, 'but not brown paper. The broom has got its feelings same as anyone else.'

'I know,' said Rosemary. 'My shoe bag!'

She ran to the wardrobe, tipped out her gym shoes, and brought it to the bed. It was made of scarlet flannel.

'Not a bad idea,' said Carbonel grudgingly, as they slipped it carefully on. Rosemary drew up the strings and tied them securely.

'What magic runes are on the side?' asked the cat suspiciously.

The words ROSEMARY BROWN were embroidered in white chain stitch. 'We have to have that, so that it won't get lost at school,' said Rosemary.

'That is the practical sort of magic that I like to see.'

By now John had completely recovered from his ride on the broom, and was bouncing up and down on the bed.

'I say, I am hungry. Let's fry those sausages.'

So they went into the sitting room. When they had mopped up the flower water which John had knocked over in his wild flight, the feast still looked pretty good. Carbonel seemed genuinely touched by the sprats which were piled up on a soup plate. Rosemary showed John how to prick the sausages and he fried everything they could find – two onions, some cold potatoes, and a slightly squashy tomato that made the fat splutter, as well as the sausages. It was a delightful meal, eaten in friendly silence, and neither of them minded that the potatoes were a bit burnt, or that all of the sausages had burst. Carbonel, replete with all the sprats and two saucers of milk, purred sleepily while they ate the cream buns (a little soggy here and there with flower water, but otherwise delicious). When they were comfortably licking the gob-stoppers, Carbonel got up, arched his back, delicately stretched first one front paw and then the other, and sat down, very upright, with his tail curled round his toes.

'I have something to tell you,' he said. 'Today I went to see my People ... Strictly incognito, of course.'

'What does that mean?' asked Rosemary.

'I think it means pretending you are not yourself,' said John.

'That was where I went the night before,' went on Carbonel, ignoring the interruption.

'Goodness!' said Rosemary. 'You never told me!'

'You never asked,' said Carbonel shortly. 'I told you that I am a Royal Cat, and that as soon as I am free I must return to my kingdom.'

'But where is your kingdom?' asked John.

'Come here and I will show you.'

Carbonel trotted into Rosemary's bedroom and jumped on to the window ledge.

'Behold!' he said dramatically. Rosemary looked down.

'Do you mean the back yard?' she asked doubtfully.

'Good gracious, no! Don't you see the roof tops, plains and valleys and canyons of them? And the forests of chimney stacks and wireless aerials stretching away

75

and away into the golden afternoon? That is my kingdom, the undisputed territory of the cats. Now look
down. What do you see?'

'The dustbins in the yard,' said John cheerfully. But
Carbonel did not seem to be listening.

'You see the garden wall stretching along the end of
all the gardens in Tottenham Grove? All walls, like
that one, are our highways. What else could they be
there for? So many humans seem to think that the proper place for a cat is on the hearth-rug. You might as
well argue that the proper place for a bird is in a cage.
No, it is on the roof tops that we are our true selves.
There we live our secret lives, there we skirmish, we
royster, we sing songs. Songs of such beauty that men
throw up their windows and shout applause.'

Rosemary was not sure that it was always applause
she had heard, but she did not say so. The houses of
Tottenham Grove were taller than the ones on to which
she looked from her bedroom window. She had always
liked the huddle of roofs, with different shaped chimney
pots, some with cowls that twisted and twirled with the
wind, some clustered together in all shapes and sizes,
and some in neat rows like sand pies on the beach. It
might almost be some strange country, she thought.
Below her she could see the top of the wall that stretched
along the back of all the smutty little gardens of Tottenham Grove, with the side walls joining it like tributaries.
She could see a couple of cats now trotting along, one of
them in a purposeful way.

'A lot of cats come into the garden,' she said.

'We colonize, of course,' said Carbonel loftily. 'But
my poor People!'

'Why, what has happened?' said John.

'When my father died,' went on the cat, 'mourned by

all his subjects, I am told – Carbonel the Good he was called (may I be worthy of him) – there was no Royal Kit to take his place, since the rightful heir had been stolen.'

'You?' asked John.

Carbonel inclined his head.

'What did they do?'

'A couple of cousins tried their hand at ruling, but what could they be expected to do? Mere tabbies. Very distant cousins they were. Well, of course, the inevitable happened. They had no proper authority, and things began to get slack, and then, of course, the Alley Cats got restless. Always on the look-out for making mischief, they are.'

'But who is King now?' asked Rosemary.

Carbonel drew himself up, and surveyed the roof tops through half-closed eyes.

'There can be no King until I return. Once a month since time immemorial we have held the Law Giving at the full moon. There my father, and his father, and his father's father before that, dispensed justice and wisdom. These fellows make a mockery of it. They brawl and fight and challenge anyone to dispute their leadership. Of course, at first there were plenty of good and bad cats to cross claws with them. They fight for it every month till the strongest one wins, the winner calls himself King, and there he sits on the throne of my fathers until the next Law Giving, when another animal will dispute his claim. A sorry, battered collection of animals go limping home, I can tell you!'

'How did you find out all this?' asked John.

'By getting into conversation with all sorts and putting two and two together. Mostly honest, decent house animals they were. There are plenty of them about, I can tell you, who are loyal to "The Cat Among the Stars", as they call me. But the Alley Cats have got the upper hand. I heard today that for the last three months the same great ginger animal has been in command. He fights like a tiger, and levies I don't know what taxes of kipper heads and sardine tins.'

'But now you can go and turn him out, and it will all be right again!' said Rosemary.

'I bet you could beat him with one ... one paw behind your back!' said John. Carbonel graciously inclined his head.

'No doubt. But what use is a King who is at the beck and call of somebody else? I am still a slave.'

'Do you mean to me?' said Rosemary. 'But I wouldn't beck and call, ever!'

'So you may think now. But power does queer things, you know. The original Binding Spell is broken. Rosemary did that when she bought me with her three Queen Victoria farthings. But there still remains the second spell, the one SHE made when I tried to escape.'

'Then we must set about finding the hat and the cauldron straight away!' said Rosemary. She felt a little uncomfortable that the fun of meeting John had made her forget how important this was to Carbonel.

'What do you do when you have got them?' asked John, who was a practical person.

'That is the worst of it. She made a Silent Magic, just to make it more difficult, so of course I never heard it. She is the only one who can tell you how to undo the spell.'

'Oh dear!' said Rosemary uneasily, thinking of the queer old woman.

'Well, I tell you what,' said John. 'When Jeffries comes to fetch us this afternoon, let's ask him to take us to that address you got at the market. You know, the man who bought the hat.'

'What a good idea! Come on, let's wash up quickly, so that we shall be ready when he comes.'

'Do we have to?' said John.

'We do,' said Rosemary firmly.

13

The Occupier

WHILE they washed up the dinner things they discussed their plans. What sort of person would have bought the witch's hat from Fairfax Market? They did not even know his name. All they had to go on was the address on the envelope with the soap powder coupon in it, and that merely said:

To the Occupier, 101 Cranshaw Road, Netherley.

'Youngish,' the old man at the second-hand stall had said he was, wearing clothes that were 'good but wore.'

'Well, anyway, the first thing is to get Jeffries to take us there,' said John. 'I expect he will. He is a friend of mine. He can waggle his ears when he's off duty. He let me help change a wheel once.'

'You'd better leave me and Broom behind,' said Carbonel. 'Best draw as little attention to us as possible, and cats and witch's besoms on buses are a bit conspicuous. You and your mother will be coming home from Tussocks by bus this time, I suppose, and it will be the rush hour.'

Jeffries was more amenable than they had dared to hope. He was a large, freckled young man who grinned readily.

'You're in luck. I know Cranshaw Road quite well. Pass it when I go to see my young lady,' he said, flushing slightly.

'Do take us there on the way home,' said John. 'Be a sport!'

'You could leave us at number hundred and one, and then go and see your young lady, say for half-an-hour. It would be a lovely surprise for her!' said Rosemary tactfully.

'What are you young limbs up to?' said Jeffries, but without malice.

'Very important business,' said John gravely. 'Look here, couldn't you leave us there for even twenty minutes?'

The prospect of seeing his young lady was more than the chauffeur could resist. He laughed. 'All right, you win!' he said, and turned the car in the direction of Netherley.

'Only half-an-hour, mind!' called Jeffries, as he left them outside number hundred and one.

It was a large, comfortable Victorian house with a circular drive leading to the front door. Above the bell were three names, which seemed to indicate that the house was divided up into flats.

'Don't let's stop to think, or I shall want not to,' said Rosemary, clutching the envelope tightly. 'Try the bottom bell.'

John nodded. He was already feeling 'want not to', but nothing would make him admit it; with the result that he rang the bell rather harder than he meant to. It rang sharply in the distance, and a rather cross-looking woman in an overall opened the door.

'Now go away,' she said sharply. ''E doesn't want any juveniles! As if I 'adn't enough to do!' she added mysteriously, and slammed the door.

Rosemary looked at John with dismay. But curiously enough with the ringing of the door bell his courage had revived.

'Well, we've come all this way, so don't let's give up

just for that. Let's explore. Look here, that gate at the side is open and I can hear someone moving about. Let's go and look.'

Cautiously they pushed one of the double doors and looked in. There was a paved yard flanked on one side by the kitchens of the house, and on the other by a building that must once have been stables, but was obviously used now as a garage. In the middle of the yard was a large, pale blue lorry, which said in newly painted scarlet letters, 'The Netherley Players'. Sticking out from under the lorry was a pair of legs in dirty grey flannel trousers. John and Rosemary advanced cautiously. They waited for a pause in the exasperated noises that were coming from underneath, and then John said: 'Excuse me, but are you the Occupier?'

And the voice that had been making exasperated noises said absently, 'Well, that depends. I don't occupy much. I'm away rather a lot. But the Briggs on the top floor are generally occupying.'

The voice went on jerkily, as though the owner was making some great effort, 'But the Pattersons might be said to occupy like mad. They've got three children.'

There was a sharp rattle, as of a spanner slipping, and a smothered exclamation, and the body belonging to the grey flannel legs squirmed into view, revealing a bright green open-necked shirt liberally smeared with oil. Rosemary supposed that the stall-holder at the Market, who was old, might consider this a 'youngish man'. He stopped sucking his bleeding knuckles long enough to say:

'But on the other hand, I am the old original Occupier. I say, what do you want to know for?'

'We've brought something back for you. You

dropped it at Fairfax Market,' and she held out the crumpled envelope.

'That's very kind of you.'

The man took the envelope and looked inside.

'What on earth is it?'

'It's a coupon that you can exchange for a large packet of Lathero for the price of a small one.'

'But what on earth should I do with a packet of Lathero when I'd bought it?'

'You could wash your shirt with it,' said Rosemary gravely. 'But you had better let me tie up your hand. It's bleeding. I've got a clean hankie here.'

'Washed, I suppose, with Lathero? You are an advertising stunt, aren't you?'

'Goodness no!' said John, as Rosemary tied up the grazed hand. 'You see, the old man said that you bought the hat.'

'Aha! The incomparable witch's hat! But look here, I don't understand. How do you know anything about it?'

'Well, you see,' said Rosemary, 'I've got the cat that belonged to the same witch, and the broom-stick.'

'On which you doubtless swept up to the front door,' said the man with a twinkle.

'Oh no, we came in Aunt Amabel's car because we didn't want to use up the broom's magic. And Jeffries – he's the chauffeur – he's coming back to fetch us in half-an-hour, because he's gone to see his young lady,' said John.

'I see,' said the youngish man. 'If you ask me, a broom is a much more civilized vehicle than a car. It doesn't have to be screwed up with spanners that turn round and hit you.' He looked ruefully at his bandaged hand. 'But look here, suppose you tell me what you

have really come for?' And he grinned so encouragingly
that Rosemary said:

'We want the witch's hat, please.'

The grin faded. There was an awkward pause,
and the man called, 'Molly, can you come here a
minute?'

A girl's voice answered, 'All right, but I shall never
finish these tunics if you keep interrupting,' and the
awkwardness was broken by the arrival of a girl in tight-
fitting slacks and a yellow sweater. She was pretty and
looked kind, Rosemary decided thankfully.

'What is it?' she inquired.

'Ask me another,' said the young man, lighting a
cigarette. 'These youngsters want the hat I bought at
Fairfax Market.'

'But what for? Look here, come upstairs, then we can
sit down and discuss it comfortably.'

They walked in procession into a garage and up some
wooden stairs into what had probably once been a hay
loft. It had a stack of wicker baskets at one end, one of
which was open, showing a jumble of coloured ma-
terials inside. There was a table near the window with a
sewing machine on it, and a pile of sewing, and on a
shelf were rows of headdresses on stands, top hats, hel-
mets, medieval headdresses with horns and veils, three-
cornered hats, and at the far end ... a black, high-
pointed hat of furry, beaver felt! 'Now sit down and tell
us all about it,' said Molly.

Cheered by her kindness and the nearness of the hat,
Rosemary sat down on a dress basket and told them the
whole story.

'So you see,' she ended up, 'we simply must have the
witch's hat or we can't do anything.'

'But look here,' said the young man when she had

done, 'of course you tell it awfully well, but you can't come here with a fairy tale like that and expect me to hand over the hat on a plate! It's a very rare thing, I don't mind telling you. It must be very old. I've half a mind to take it to Fairfax Museum and see what they think of it.'

Rosemary was aghast. 'Oh, don't do that. They might put it in a glass case, and we should never get it then.'

'You certainly wouldn't,' said the young man shortly.

'But we only want to borrow it, you know.'

'Now look here ...' began the young man crossly, when Molly interrupted.

'No, Bill, leave it to me. Tomorrow morning we are going off on tour. Bill and I, and some others, of course, act plays. We go round to village halls and schools and things, and we must have the hat to take with us. There isn't time to get another, let alone make one. You see that, don't you?' Rosemary and John nodded.

'Now suppose you wait until you have got the cauldron, and all this Silent Magic taped, and perhaps we might lend it to you then, just for the final spell. What about that for a solution?'

'Oh thank you!' said Rosemary gratefully. 'You are kind! We shan't forget, shall we, John? And you will take great care of the hat, won't you?'

'Great care. I promise. Perhaps you could come and see us act. Bill, give them a handbill. That will show you where we are going to be.'

'Then we shall know where to find you when we are ready to borrow the hat,' said John.

'So you will, *when* you are ready,' said the young man.

85

'Thank you very much. But I think we ought to go now; Jeffries will be waiting.'

So they all shook hands, and Molly and the young man saw them to the car, where a slightly anxious Jeffries was waiting for them. They had been a good deal longer than half-an-hour.

14

Making Plans

JOHN and Rosemary reached Tussocks in time for tea. Mrs Pendlebury Parker was out, so they asked if they might have theirs on two trays so that they could take them where they liked in the garden.

'Let's have it on the stone seat,' said Rosemary.

It had been a hot, sunny day, and the seat was warm to sit on. There were fat cushions of moss and little plants growing between the paving stones at their feet, and the yellow roses above dropped slow petals on to their tea-trays.

'I feel like a princess,' said Rosemary.

'You don't look like one. You've lost one of your hair ribbons.'

'Bother!' said Rosemary. 'You know, I think this afternoon was pretty satisfactory. The Occupier man, I mean. And I liked Molly, too. They promised to take care of the hat, and now we know from the handbill exactly where they are going to be, so that all we've got to do is to write and ask them for it when we are ready. You can have the rest of my cucumber sandwiches. I like the scrunch when you bite them, but I don't like the taste much.'

'I hope it's all right, about the hat, I mean,' said John doubtfully. 'The trouble is you never can tell with grown-ups. You know how they say "Not today, dear, another time!" when you know perfectly well that that's simply a polite way of saying "No, you jolly well can't!"'

'Oh dear, I hadn't thought of that,' said Rosemary. 'All the same, it would be best to do as Molly suggested. I mean get the cauldron and the Silent Magic ready first, and then try again for the hat.'

John nodded. His mouth was too full to speak. Presently he said, 'I say, we've got an awful lot to do. It will be hard enough to find the witch, let alone get her to tell us the spell.'

Remembering the strange old woman, Rosemary wriggled uneasily. 'I know. You wait till you meet her!'

'Well, I've been thinking. We can't get on with anything much unless we can get more time on our own. I tell you what I'll do. Mummy said she was going to ring up Aunt Amabel tonight, and she is sure to talk to me, too. I'll tell her about you ...'

'Not about the magic,' interrupted Rosemary. 'I don't think it is wise to talk about that unless we've got to. The Occupier went all queer and cautious when he saw we really meant it – about the magic, I mean. And he was so nice before that. Didn't you notice?'

John nodded. 'I won't say anything about magic, only you. We're allowed to do pretty well what we like at home during the holidays ... if there are two of us. I can say we want to explore the old town, go to Fairfax Museum, and the cathedral and things like that, and she will speak to Aunt Amabel about it. Aunt Amabel thinks you are a "quaint, ladylike little thing". I heard her say so. Of course,' he went on reassuringly, 'I know you aren't anything of the kind, but she meant it as a compliment, so I expect it will be all right.'

The sky had clouded over, and great drops of rain were beginning to fall as well as rose petals. So they picked up their trays and ran indoors.

'It was nice of John to come and thank me for letting

him come to dinner,' said Mrs Brown on the way home in the bus. 'It quite cheered up my curtain making.'

'Poor Mummy! Is it being horribly dull, the curtain making and sides to middling? It doesn't seem fair when I'm having such a gorgeous time!'

Her mother laughed. 'Then I don't mind a bit. I'm glad you are enjoying it, darling. I was afraid they were going to be such dull holidays for you. Mrs Pendlebury Parker wants you to play with John every day it can be managed. Will you like that?'

'I shall love it!' said Rosemary.

She had no opportunity of talking to Carbonel until she went to bed that night.

'Well, I suppose you've learnt something,' he said rather grudgingly, when she had told him all about the day's adventures, 'even if it's only when to hold your tongue with human grown-ups. Still, to be fair, the temptation to say the Summoning Words and produce *me* must have been overpowering,' he added complacently.

He was washing the difficult part under his chin as he sat beside her on the bed, and broke off to say:

'On the whole you managed quite creditably.' He transferred his attention to his right hind leg, and went on between licks:

'I put in a little social time with Mrs Walker. I must say I like her taste in hearth rugs – very cosy. I collected some more talk about the Alley Cats. Heartrending, it is, the damage they are doing. Even the Humans are noticing. The tabby next door has got a torn ear and the grey at the tobacconist's has been taken to the Vet. Now, if you and John can get about a bit on your own, Broom and I can go with you, and then we really shall begin to get somewhere.'

Rosemary swallowed her annoyance at his patronizing tone.

'I suppose it is hateful for you, Carbonel. I mean, being "minion of the twiggy broom", and me!'

'Somehow it's harder to be so near my liberty than it was when I was with HER, and there seemed no hope of release. It might be much worse, I keep telling myself. You are kind, and really quite intelligent for a human, and you stroke very well indeed.' He was purring now, deep, slow, regular purrs. 'So you must not mind if I'm a bit sharp now and then.'

In answer, Rosemary lifted him bodily into her lap. She was sitting cross-legged on her bed, and he settled into the hollow of her nightdress like water into a bowl. His yellow eyes were the merest slits of gold. For a while she sat in the dusk listening to the diminishing purr, then she said softly:

'Dear Carbonel! We will get you free as soon as ever we can.'

There was no reply. The purr had faded into silence. Carbonel was asleep.

15

Where is the cauldron?

I T was two days later before they were actually able to set out together on their own. They each had an extra shilling and a packet of sandwiches which the cook at Tussocks had made up for them. Rosemary carried the broom, and Carbonel trotted in front with his tail erect.

'We've got hours and hours!' said John happily. 'How glorious! All the same, don't let's waste time by walking to the Market. Let's go by bus.'

Business people had already gone to their offices, and only a few shopping ladies were out so early, so they had the front seat and the top of the bus to themselves. They swayed and rocked through the narrow streets, as John said, like a galleon in a stormy sea. They were so busy sailing the Spanish Main with sailors dying of scurvy like flies round them, that they reached the terminus before they knew where they were. They had agreed that the best thing to do was to go and find the friendly old man who had seen Mrs Cantrip selling her things, and ask him if he remembered who had bought the cauldron. But as they had told Mrs Pendlebury Parker that they would go and see the Museum, it seemed wisest to go there first and 'get it over', as John said, rather as if it was a visit to the dentist.

The Museum was a large house which overlooked the Market. It was very old, and full of unexpected corners, and the floors ran up and down in a pleasantly disconcerting way. Although she did not like to say so for fear of sounding priggish, Rosemary rather liked looking at museums. But in spite of himself, John found he was getting really interested. There were suits of armour, and swords and halberds and ancient pistols with beautifully inlaid handles. There was a sedan chair with a window that let up and down like a window in a railway carriage, there was a very large glove that had belonged to Queen Elizabeth I which was embroidered all over with flowers and animals, and some early Victorian dresses that Rosemary would have loved to dress up in, and a case of battered dolls that bore all the marks of having been well and truly played with.

'I always think that things that were meant to be used look rather sad all shut up in a museum, just to be looked at,' said Rosemary.

They were passing through a long room that had been built on at the back to house the Wilkinson Collection of china, which the attendant told them was one of the finest in the country. 'Just look at all these tea-sets! It must be horrid for them never to be poured out of for people to have nice cosy tea-parties.'

'Pooh! Dull, old grown-up talk!' said John. 'I think we have seen most of the museum now, so let's go to the Market.'

Rosemary would like to have stayed longer, but she followed John out into the sunshine with a feeling of relief that they need no longer talk in whispers. Carbonel was sunning himself on the steps outside with the broom propped up in a corner beside him. Rosie led the way to the friendly old man. When they reached the stall, a fat woman was haggling over some linoleum. When she had gone off with a large roll of it under her arm, the old man noticed Rosemary.

'Hallo, Susie,' he said. 'Them fairy wands still ain't

come in. I'm expecting a couple of gross any day now!'
And he laughed wheezily at his own joke.

Rosemary laughed politely, too. If she could get him
to go on treating it as a joke she could go straight to the
point.

'It's not a fairy wand I want this time. It's a witch's
cauldron.'

'A cauldron, eh? Well, you could cook up a tidy spell
in that fish-kettle over there!' And he went off into a fit
of wheezing that quite alarmed Rosemary.

'Oh, but it must be one of those black things with a
handle over the top. That's what witches always use.'

'There's not much call for them these days,' said the
old man, dropping into his professional manner once
more, 'not since people 'ave begun to go in for these
new-fangled grates, and gas and electricity. The only
coal-scuttles they want are the kind you just tip the coals
on with so as not to dirty yer 'ands. Now where did I
see one of those things lately? Now wasn't it you I was
telling about the old party that set up next to me and
sold 'er 'at? Well, believe it or not, she'd got one of
them old coal-scuttles, too.'

'Did she sell it?' asked Rosemary cautiously.

'Must 'ave,' said the old man. 'I don't think I saw
'oo to, because I was busy with a customer over 'alf a
dozen spoons. Stop a bit, though . . . I remember, now,
seeing a stout party walking away with it.'

'I remember you saying you could read people's
clothes like a book, being in the trade, you said.'

The old man's eye lit up.

'A regular Sherlock 'Olmes, that's me! Artistic that
one was. I remember I says to myself, " 'andwoven,
good but baggy, skirt and jacket twenty-five bob."
She'd got grey 'air done in them buns that flap over 'er

ears. It's a funny thing, I've got it into my 'ead she said she kept a shop. Must 'ave said something about it, I reckon, but I can't recall what.'

'What could she have wanted the cauldron for?' asked John.

'You never know with that sort,' said the old man darkly. 'Not without it was for coal.' And he turned his attention to a sad-looking young man who wanted to buy some gramophone records.

The children wandered off and sat down on an old packing case.

'Now the thing is,' said John, 'what kind of shop would an artistic sort of grey-haired lady run?'

'There are quite a lot of shops near the Cathedral that sell hand-made things and souvenirs,' said Rosemary. 'They are mostly kept by people like that.'

'I believe you are right,' said Carbonel. 'The Cathedral is not far.'

'I vote we eat our sandwiches in the grassy part round it, then we shouldn't have to lug them about with us,' said John. 'Isn't it funny how food seems to stop being heavy once it's inside you? I suppose it's something to do with balance.'

They walked to the Cathedral and sat on a seat outside with the sun casting the shadow of the great golden-grey building across the green grass, and the rooks cawing and circling overhead. The Cathedral clock over the west door struck eleven. It was a fascinating clock, with two fat little angels standing on either side with hammers, with which they beat the hours and the quarters on a bell. By the time the angels had struck the half-hour John and Rosemary had eaten their sausage rolls and scrambled egg sandwiches. Carbonel had one filled with anchovy paste which Rosemary had brought

They walked to the Cathedral and sat on a seat.

specially for him. By the time the angels had struck twelve the children had finished their pieces of cake and a bag of fat red gooseberries. Carbonel was pacing impatiently up and down, to the annoyance of the sparrows, who watched with eager eyes the crumbs that Rosemary shook from her lap.

'What a fuss humans have to make over everything,' the cat said scornfully as they collected the sandwich papers and turned to look for a rubbish basket. 'We don't go picking up our fishbones when we've eaten the fish. We just eat the bones as well. Tidy and economical.'

'Well, I'm blowed if I'm going to eat all this greaseproof paper,' said John. 'Come on, let's try all the artistic-looking shops at the top of the High Street in turn.'

There certainly were at least six likely shops which had arisen like cream to the top of the highway, where it widened in front of the Cathedral.

'Now wait a minute,' said John. 'What are we going to say when we get inside? We can't go blinding in and just demand to see their coal scuttles.'

'I tell you what,' said Rosemary. 'Let's take it in turns to engage the people in conversation, like they do in books, and find out what sort of fires they have. You don't want coal scuttles if you have gas or electric fires.'

'You are not an unintelligent child,' said Carbonel. Rosemary blushed with pleasure. He went on, 'I will listen carefully, and if they say "Coal", go on engaging them in conversation and I will slip round the counter and see if I can spot the cauldron anywhere about.'

'All right,' said Rosemary. 'Bags I the first shop, because I thought of it!'

The shop at the end of the little terrace which faced the Cathedral was called 'The Bijouterie'. The window was full of brooches made of fishbones, and boxes and ash-trays ornamented with barbola. There was a big pot of dried poppy heads enamelled red and blue. Rosemary went inside before she had really thought how you 'engage people in conversation'. Characters in books never explain how this is done – they seem to be born knowing how to do it. The woman behind the counter said briskly, 'Yes, dear, what do you want?'

She was a thin person in an embroidered peasant blouse, with her hair cut in a fringe. Rosemary's mind went quite blank. She stood stupidly just looking, while she thought of something to say. Only at a hissed 'Go on!' from John, who was standing by the doorway with the broom, did she rouse herself. Pointing to a tray of postcards she gulped, 'Please may I look at these?'

'Sixpence each,' said the woman. 'They are done by a local artist. So much nicer than a photo, I always think.'

Rosemary looked at them doubtfully. Sixpence seemed a lot of money to pay for a postcard, and the pictures were so fuzzy that it was difficult to tell what they were about. She looked at them in rather desperate silence. Finally she chose one that she did recognize as the Market Cross, and regretfully handed over sixpence. Carbonel rubbed himself against her bare legs. He could not talk to her, because she had not got the broom, but she knew quite well what he meant. Rosemary took a deep breath and said:

'What lovely weather! Not ... not at all the sort of day for sitting by the fire!'

The woman looked a little surprised but agreed politely, adding – as if she knew what they wanted to discover – 'Leastways, not with gas the price it is. Though I must say I like a bit of fire in the evenings.'

Rosemary took the card and ran out of the shop, where John was waiting.

'Gas!' she said triumphantly, and showed John the postcard.

'I thought we could send it to your sister. It's not that way up, silly! It cost sixpence.'

'Well, the artist shouldn't have done it on a day when there was such a thick fog. I say, you did look funny when you just stood there gawping.'

'Well, I found out, anyway. It's your turn now.'

There was a great number of brass ornaments in the next shop – door knockers and nut crackers and ash trays and little bells made like ladies with crinoline skirts, and proverbs like 'Every cloud has a silver lining' done in poker work. John handed the broom over to Rosemary and marched in. A tall thin man was flicking a shelf full of china ornaments with a feather duster.

'Can you tell me the price of those brass toasting forks, please?' said John.

'Ten and six,' said the man, turning from his dusting.

'Oh,' said John. 'The thing is that the uncle I have in mind is rather fussy about his toast. He might not like it made with a brass toasting fork. He always insists on a coal fire to make it by, because he says it tastes so much better.'

'Well, I swear by electric,' said the man. 'We've got one of those things that shoots the toast out when it's done.'

'Don't you ever make it by a coal fire?'

'We haven't got one in the house. My wife says they're dirty. Though I must say they are more homey.'

'Just what I think,' said John. 'Do you know, on the

whole I think perhaps my uncle wouldn't like his toast made with brass, so I won't get the toasting fork. But thank you all the same,' and John left the shop.

'You see, it's quite easy, really,' he said cockily, 'and I didn't spend any money.'

'Well, I don't think you ought to have made up all that stuff about your uncle,' said Rosemary.

'I didn't,' said John virtuously. 'I have got an uncle who is fussy about his toast. Go on. You had better do that embroidery shop at the corner, and if you must buy something, get photographs of the cathedral, they're cheaper.'

But here they drew a blank. The woman in charge had several customers and refused to be engaged in conversation. The children persevered, going from one shop to another with varying success, and wherever they found someone who owned to having a coal fire Carbonel padded silently behind the counter. Once or twice he was shooed ignominiously out. Working their way down the High Street, they passed the Town Hall and the Cottage Hospital, right down to the railway station, where there were only offices and a few little shops that sold newspapers and tobacco. By this time they had inquired at eleven shops. It was well into the afternoon, and they felt tired, hot, and discouraged. Not a trace of the cauldron had they found.

'I can't go another step!' said Rosemary. 'It feels hours since we had our sandwiches. I tell you what. We passed a tea shop a little farther back where p'raps we could sit down and have ices. I've got sixpence of my shilling left, and threepence of my pocket money.'

John was only too willing, so they retraced their steps and went into the tea shop. It was called the Copper Kettle, and there was a beautifully polished kettle in the window flanked by plates of home-made cakes. Lunch had been cleared away, and a young woman in a chintz overall was laying tables for tea. The walls were panelled with what looked like oak, and it was cool and pleasant inside. The large strawberry ices slid like nectar down their thirsty throats. The children found that by putting the broom on the floor underneath the table, and slipping off a sandal each, so that their bare feet rested on the handle, they could both hear what Carbonel had to say at the same time. He sat under the table to be as inconspicuous as possible.

'I've just thought of something awful!' said Rosemary. 'Suppose the artistic lady didn't want to use the cauldron as a coal-scuttle at all? Then it doesn't matter what sort of fires all those people have, and our whole day has been wasted.'

'Golly!' said John, so appalled by this idea that he stopped with a spoon full of ice-cream half-way to his mouth. 'You mean that they may be using the cauldron for ... well, standing ferns ... or bathing the baby?'

'Not in the shops we went to,' said Carbonel from under the table. 'Most of them had a cat of some kind, and I took the precaution of getting into conversation in most places. Quite civil most of them were. One of 'em even gave me her saucer of milk which, considering that strawberry ice-cream doesn't seem to be coming my way, is just as well.' And if a cat could sniff, that is what Carbonel would have done.

'But Carbonel, darling! Would you like ice-cream?' asked Rosemary in distress.

'Not a bit. But I should like to be asked,' he said in an injured voice.

Rosemary held a dab of ice-cream under the table on

her finger. Carbonel licked it off, but it made him sneeze.

'We seem to have spent an awful lot of money,' said John.

'I didn't seem able to engage people in conversation unless I bought something,' said Rosemary. 'Do you think your sister will like nine photographs of the cathedral?' she asked anxiously.

'The postage would cost one and sixpence, so I shall do them up in brown paper and send them for tuppence ha'-penny. She will probably think I've gone potty,' he added gloomily, scraping the last drops of runny ice-cream from the edges of the dish. 'Well, what on earth do we do now?'

16

The cauldron

THERE was a gloomy silence while they tried to think what would be the best thing to do. Rosemary was the first to speak.

'Well, I think ...' she began. But she never said what she thought, because it was then it happened.

Shopping ladies with parcels were beginning to come in for an early tea, and the chintz-overalled waitress was hurrying past their table with a tray laden with tea things when she caught her foot against the broom, tottered for one horrifying moment and fell with a crash. The shopping ladies stopped talking and turned round. John and Rosemary jumped up and helped her to her feet. Rosie began to pick up the broken china, and tried to rescue the cakes and buttered toast that were lying forlornly in a lake of tea.

'I'm so awfully sorry!' said Rosemary in distress. 'I do hope you did not hurt yourself? Do sit down for a minute.'

'We will clear it all up,' said John. 'I'm afraid it was our fault.'

'I should think it was!' said the waitress crossly. 'And I don't know what Maggie will say to all this broken china! Why couldn't you put your walking stick in the umbrella stand by the door?' She rubbed her bruised shin as she spoke.

'Look!' whispered Rosemary to John. 'Look over there!'

John turned and stared in the same direction as Rosemary. Peering anxiously round the door that led to the kitchen, was a plump, elderly woman with hair plaited in two buns, one over each ear. She was wearing an apron, but under it was an obviously hand-woven jacket.

'Are you all right, Florrie?' she said anxiously, and then she saw the mess on the floor and gave a moan. 'The china, Florrie. How could you!'

By this time the broken tea things had been collected on the tray.

'Please sit down, ladies,' she went on. 'I will bring you more tea in a minute. Florrie, you had better get a cloth.'

'Let me get it, because it was our fault,' said Rosemary. 'Don't do that!' she said to John, who had dug her rather hard in the ribs. But all that John said was, 'Look at Carbonel!'

The black cat was standing near the door that led to the street, his tail straight up in the air and his back arched, kneading the matting with his front paws and making strange crooning noises in his throat.

'What is the matter with him?' asked Rosemary anxiously. But John was staring as fixedly as Carbonel.

'Over there in the corner! The umbrella stand!'

In the corner by the door, holding two umbrellas and a walking stick, was a fat black pot with three legs, and a handle over the top.

'It's the witch's cauldron, isn't it?' breathed Rosemary.

The cat was quiet now. He turned and stalked towards them with his head held high.

'Of course it is. I'd know it anywhere, even got up like that!'

Its well-rounded sides gleamed with black lead, and

the copper band round it had been polished till it glowed.

'Besides,' he went on, 'there is the patch in the bottom where it began to leak. Well, what are we waiting for? You had better pick it up and get out while this to-do is going on.'

Rosemary was shocked.

'We can't just take it! That would be stealing. We must think of a plan for getting it honestly somehow. But first we must help to clear up. You collect the buttered toast that skidded over there, and I'll go and fetch another cloth.'

She hurried through the door into the kitchen. The waitress passed her coming out with a dust-pan and brush, and only the one she had referred to as Maggie was there. She looked up as Rosemary came in.

'Go away, little girl. As if you had not done enough damage for today!'

'I know,' said Rosemary penitently. 'It's because I'm so sorry about it that I thought I'd come and get a cloth and help to clear up. I will polish the floor again when it's dry if you will let me.'

'It's not the floor that matters, it's the china.'

There was a quiver in the woman's voice, and to Rosemary's horror her round face suddenly crumpled and she began to cry.

'Oh, don't!' said Rosemary. 'Don't cry, please! Whatever is the matter? Do tell me, and then I'm sure it will make you feel better. I've got a clean hankie somewhere, I know I have.'

The woman did not take the handkerchief, but she stopped crying and wiped her eyes with her own.

'It's the china,' she said jerkily, as she dabbed at her face. 'The girls we have hired to wash up broke so much that we decided to try and manage without them, and besides that we couldn't really afford to go on paying their wages. Business has been so bad lately. Florrie and I are on our feet all day, but it is no use. And because there were only the two of us we needed so much more china because the washing up was slower.'

'But why don't you buy some more?' asked Rosemary.

'Because we haven't enough money, and neither of the china shops will give us any more credit. But I don't know why I'm telling you all this!' She gave a watery smile and dabbed at her face again with her handkerchief. 'There is a big Women's Institute rally this afternoon at the Temperance Hall, and I'd hoped for quite a lot of customers. The cakes are made all ready. But what is the use of customers if we have not enough china for them to eat off?' Miss Maggie sniffed ominously again.

'I see,' said Rosemary slowly. 'You mean that if you had more china, quite a lot of it, that you would earn a great deal of money this afternoon?'

'I'd give anything I've got for some more china. You see, that's not all.'

'Oh dear. Is there some more?' Miss Maggie nodded.

'This afternoon my brother was coming to see how we are getting on. He put up the money for the tea shop in the first place, and if he sees that we're busy he will probably help us out a bit, but if he thinks it is being a failure he'll say it's throwing good money after bad. Oh, well,' she went on, 'it's no use bothering you with our troubles.' And she turned heavily to the sink, looking so dejected that Rosemary said:

'Oh, please cheer up. I might be able to help. About the china, I mean. But I must talk to my friends first.'

She ran out of the kitchen, to find John waiting impatiently for her.

'What have you been doing all this time?' he asked crossly.

'Hush, I'll tell you. Come outside, quickly!'

They hurried out and turned down a little passage that ran down the side of the shop.

'Carbonel,' said Rosemary. 'Now we have got the cauldron, can it do some magic – grant wishes and things?'

Carbonel considered. 'It's a bit irregular. You don't belong to the Sinister Sisterhood, but the cauldron might do it to oblige me. But what for?'

Rosemary told them about the Women's Institute rally, and the broken china, and the brother who was not going to throw good money after bad, and then she added:

'. . . And Miss Maggie said that she would give everything she had got if she had enough china for this afternoon. So you see, if we could help I believe she would let us have the cauldron.'

Carbonel trotted off without a word.

17

The Wishing Magic

In a few minutes Carbonel was back again, looking very pleased with himself.

'It's all right. I've persuaded it to do just one Wishing Magic to oblige. It's a bit risky on account of the poor thing really being a bit past it, what with the Pot Mender, and so on. But it will do what it can.'

'How exciting!' said John. 'What do we do?'

'Well, wishing spells are Rainbow Magic. But, of course, you know that?'

John and Rosemary both shook their heads. 'You don't? Good gracious! That's how the story began that there is a pot of gold at the foot of the rainbow, simply because gold is what so many people wish for. The whole tale is just superstition, but that is how it started. Well, of course we must make a Rainbow Brew. Can you do that, do you think?'

Again Rosemary shook her head. 'But I'll do anything you tell me to!'

'I can't think what they teach you at school,' said the cat severely. 'Every Witch's Kitten knows how to do that. You mix seven liquids of the seven colours of the rainbow. It doesn't much matter what, so long as the colours are right. That is why they let the kittens do it. And then, when it's nicely simmering, you say the Wishing Words ... if only I can remember them. I've heard HER say them often enough.'

Carbonel sat down with his tail neatly curled round his paws and closed his eyes.

'Oh, don't go to sleep now,' said John, dancing with impatience. The cat opened his eyes very wide.

'Who's going to sleep? Do you imagine that every time a cat closes its eyes that it is sleeping? That's when we think our deepest thoughts. Besides, how else can I concentrate, with you jigging up and down like a bobbin on a string? I think I can remember the Words all right. Now where can we do it? We can't do even the most elementary magic in the middle of the High Street in comfort.'

'When I was in the kitchen, I think I saw a sort of wash house place across the yard outside the window. Would that do?' asked Rosemary. 'I expect this passage leads into the yard.'

They went to look, and sure enough, there were some neglected-looking out-buildings.

'I'll go and get the cauldron,' said John. 'I hope to goodness no one sees me. Lucky thing it's just by the door. Rosie, you had better go and buy the rainbow things. I don't think I should be much good at that. We must keep our fares home, but you had better take the rest of my money.'

'What colours must I get?' asked Rosemary.

'The colours of the rainbow, of course,' said Carbonel. 'Red, orange, yellow, green, blue, indigo, and violet. Meet us in the wash house as soon as you can.' And he and John hurried down the passage.

They found that the wash house was a derelict building, with the sky showing through the slates here and there. There was a broken chair and some odd pots and pans and a copper in one corner. Beneath the small-paned window was an old sink with a tap and, better still, on the draining board was an ancient gas ring attached to a snake-like pipe.

'We're in luck, my boy!' said Carbonel. 'Every modern convenience. The thing is, have you got any matches?'

John went rather red, because he was not supposed to carry matches about, and he had to admit that he had one of those cardboard books. It had a portrait of a famous cricketer on the flap. He had meant to tear off the portrait and leave the matches behind, but somehow he had not.

'See if the tap works!' said Carbonel.

It worked all right. In fact, water spurted out of all sorts of unexpected places when it was turned on. They stood the gas ring on the sink, among the dust and bits of plaster, and put the half-filled cauldron over it. Then they lit the gas. It made an alarming 'pop', but by the time a breathless Rosemary had returned with a large paper bag the water was beginning to boil.

'I've got them!' she said triumphantly. 'I hope they will do!' and she tipped the things out into the sink. 'I've got lemonade powder for yellow, a packet of orange dye, a blue bag, a little bottle of green setting lotion (I got that cheap because the cap is cracked), some methylated spirits, and a bottle of indigo ink. I couldn't get all packets of dye because I hadn't enough money. Oh, and the woman in the shop let me have a pennyworth of hundreds and thousands. I thought we could add those as a sort of "thank you" to the cauldron.'

'That is just the sort of attention it will appreciate,' said Carbonel as he counted over the colours. 'Wait a minute, though. You have not got anything red.'

Rosemary's face fell. 'Oh dear! I've only got three ha'-pence left and it's getting so late! What shall I do?'

'I know,' said John. 'Nip into the kitchen and warn

Miss Maggie about the china coming, and see if there is anything red there. It isn't stealing, really, because it's for them.'

Rosemary hurried to the kitchen where Miss Maggie was arranging the half-dozen tea sets that were left. She was still sniffing slightly.

'It's all right, please cheer up! Because I think we can find you some china, as a lend, you know, for the afternoon. And then you will be able to make a lot of money with all the Women's Instituters, and your brother will be frightfully impressed!'

Miss Maggie gave a wan smile. 'You are a kind little thing, but whoever would lend us enough china? And besides, it is half past three already!'

'Goodness!' said Rosemary, 'we must hurry up. But I am almost sure we can do it, so do have a whole lot of cakes ready!'

Miss Maggie shook her head despondently, but as she turned to lift a tin from its shelf, Rosemary snatched something from the table and dashed back to the wash house with her pigtails flapping excitedly.

'I've got it, something red! A bottle of cochineal!'

The other things were already in the cauldron which Carbonel was stirring with a rung from the broken chair.

'It's making a lovely magic sort of smell already,' said John, peering gingerly into the cauldron. 'I suppose it's the setting lotion and the methylated spirits.'

Carbonel stoppped stirring, and the swirling mixture subsided into a slow simmer which made a rhythmical 'plopping' noise. 'It's about ready. Now the minute that you pour in the last thing, that's the red stuff, repeat what I say and then add what your wish is ... in rhyme if you can do it, and mind you say exactly what you mean this time!'

Rosemary nodded, breathing rather hard. She had already thought out a rhyme. This time she was determined there should be no mistake. She took a deep breath. 'I'm ready. Shall I pour in the cochineal?'

Carbonel nodded. Silently they watched while she tipped the little bottle until it was quite empty, and as the last drop fell the cauldron began to bubble furiously, seething and frothing, until a pile of rainbow-coloured bubbles rose up from the mouth.

'Say after me!' whispered Carbonel:

> *Prism,*
> > *Schism,*
> > > *Solecism.*
> *Spectrum,*
> > *Plectrum,*
> > > *Bright electrum.*
> *Knelling,*
> > *Belling,*
> > > *Wishing spelling!*

And as Rosemary repeated the last word the bubbles subsided, and an urgent boiling took their place.

'Now!' hissed Carbonel. 'Say your wish!'

Rosemary stood up very straight and said:

> *Listen to my wishing rhyme,*
> *Please bring here till closing time,*
> *All the china you can find,*
> *Of every sort and shape and kind*
> *From the Wilkinson Bequest,*
> *And John and I will do the rest!*

With a hiss and a cloud of steam that seemed to fill the wash house, the cauldron boiled over and put out the gas. For a moment they could see nothing but a fog of steam, but as it cleared they realized that something had happened.

'Good old cauldron, it's done it!' said John. And it had. The sink, the floor, the draining board, the window ledge, every shelf and corner was covered with china, rare and exquisite china, Spode china, Rockingham china, Dresden china, Chelsea china, dinner sets, banqueting sets, tea sets, jugs, ornaments, statuettes, vases. In fact it was exactly what Rosemary had asked for – all the china from the Wilkinson Bequest out of the Fairfax Museum.

'Gosh!' said John, 'you've overdone it a bit, haven't you? I mean to say, all these banqueting sets ...?'

'I have a bit,' said Rosemary as she rescued a priceless Georgian footbath from slipping off the broken chair. 'I really meant tea-sets, but if it all goes back at closing time it won't really matter,' and she darted off to the kitchen.

'Miss Maggie, Miss Maggie!' she called. 'Do come! We've done it! Heaps and heaps of china in the wash house, do come and see!' and she took the astonished Miss Maggie by the hand and ran with her across the yard. The china was still there. John was already sorting out the tea-sets from the rest. Miss Maggie's eyes were like saucers.

'But where did it come from? I did not hear it arrive. Why, it is exquisite, beautiful china! It's far too good.'

'Oh, never mind!' said Rosemary, who was jumping up and down with impatience, 'it is yours until closing time. Do think of your brother's good money after bad and the Women's Instituters. They'll be here any minute now!'

Miss Maggie took a deep breath. Then she said in an

entirely different voice, 'Florrie, go and fetch all the trays you can lay hands on, and put all the kettles on to boil, and then run round to Osbornes and buy up all the buns and scones they've got. We shall be able to pay them this evening!'

They collected all the china they could and staggered into the kitchen. The meeting at the Temperance Hall was clearly over. In the tea shop there was not an empty seat.

'Oh dear!' said Miss Florrie, 'they are getting impatient. I know all the signs.'

'Never mind, we'll help all we can,' said John, 'if you will tell us what to do.'

'Will you put all the tea pots on the rack above the stove to warm, and the little girl could arrange the tea trays on the big table, and I will go and take some orders.'

Goodness, how they worked! First they carried trays in, and then they collected dirty china and brought it back to wash up, and as fast as one customer got up to go another would take her place. And the Women's Institute ladies ate cream buns and crumpets off plates of priceless porcelain, and they drank thick, tea-shop tea from tea pots made for a Chinese Emperor when our ancestors were running about in woad.

John and Rosemary stood over the sink washing-up until they thought their backs would break.

'We've jolly well earned that old cauldron!' said John, wiping his crimson face. 'Did you see that when the brother came there was a queue outside the shop waiting to come in?'

'I know,' said Rosemary, 'isn't it splendid! He said that as they were so busy he would come back and talk to them after six.'

She stood up and pushed back her plaits for the fiftieth time.

'Talking of closing time,' said John, 'if we are not back in Tottenham Grove by six when Jeffries comes to fetch me, Aunt Amabel will be cross, and then she may not let us go off on our own again.'

Miss Maggie came in with a loaded tray which she put down on the table.

'Whew!' she said. 'It is slackening off now. I've never known such a day!'

'Isn't it splendid!' said Rosemary. 'But John and I think we ought to be going home now.'

'My dear child, I simply don't know how to thank you both. Goodness knows why you have done all you have. Where shall I return all this beautiful china? I should so like to thank the kind owner who lent it so generously. He must be rather an eccentric person.'

'You really can't thank him ... it is ... I mean he is very shy and retiring. And don't bother about returning the china. It will ... I mean, transport has been arranged!'

'And it is quite easy to repay us,' said John, who felt that in her efforts to explain things truthfully Rosemary was rather losing sight of their real object.

'My dears, anything I can do, you have only to say what you want!'

'Then would you let us have the cauldron that you use as an umbrella stand? As ... as a sort of keepsake?'

'Why, you funny little things, if that is really what you want! What an odd choice! I only paid five shillings for it in the market. Such an odd old woman I bought it from. And, of course, if you ever want tea or an ice-cream you will always be welcome at the Copper Kettle!'

John and Rosemary took off their aprons, fetched the broom and the cauldron, and said 'Goodbye'. They had had no time for any tea, so Miss Florrie put a large bag of cakes in the cauldron for them to eat in the bus.

'Goodbye, Miss Maggie. Just put the china together … and it will be collected. Goodbye, Miss Florrie!' and with yet another wave from the two sisters they set off down the High Street to the bus terminus, carrying the cauldron between them, and with Carbonel behind.

Rosemary gave a great sigh. 'Well, we've done it!'

'So we have, but I never want to see a tea towel again!' said John. 'You got off pretty lightly!' he said to the cat.

'I did what I could,' said Carbonel with dignity. 'I washed up milk jugs until I was too full to lick so much as a teaspoon of cream.'

*

'What an odd thing!' said Mrs Brown that evening. She and Rosemary had finished their supper and she was reading a copy of the evening paper which she had bought on the way home. 'Just listen to this!'

MUSEUM MYSTERY

While going on his usual rounds of the Fairfax Museum in the normal course of his duties, at 3.45 this afternoon, the attendant, Mr Arthur Pettigrew, discovered that the whole of the valuable Wilkinson Bequest China Collection had apparently been stolen. On being questioned, Mr Pettigrew said that when he left the room at 3.30 with a party of visitors everything was in its place. The police were at once informed. The theft was at first put down to a gang of thieves who have been at work in this neighbourhood, but the mystery deepened when it was discovered that all the glass cases were still locked, the keys never having left the possession of Mr Jones, the Curator. But on glancing into the room at closing time, Mr Pettigrew found that all the china had been returned, each piece being back in its right place. The theory that it was not a theft but a practical joke is strengthened by the fact that on several plates were signs of jam, and crumbs of cake and bread and butter, and that several teapots contained tea that was still quite warm.

'Did you see the Wilkinson China when you and John were at the Museum this morning?'

Rosemary nodded. 'It was all there when we went to see it,' she said quite truthfully.

18

Where is she?

ON the way home from the Copper Kettle, John and
Rosemary had discussed their next move. They had got
together the broom and the cauldron, and the hat, they
felt, was theirs for the asking. The next thing to do was
to find Mrs Cantrip and persuade her to tell them what
was the Silent Magic which would free Carbonel finally
and completely. It was not until three days later that
they felt they could ask to go off on their own again;
three days spent pleasantly enough playing in the garden at Tussocks. It was Carbonel who urged them to
hurry. He grew daily more restless and, truth to tell,
more cantankerous. Rosemary would sit at her window
in the evenings and watch with renewed interest the cat
world that trotted so purposefully along the garden
walls and over the leads and slates beyond. She would
stare at the chimneys and roofs, some sloping steeply,
some with a gradual incline, with here and there a
tower or steeple standing above them, until in the half
light the harsh lines of slate and brick seemed to soften
and undulate, like living hills and valleys. The evening
smoke from the chimney-pots wreathed itself mysteriously round them. Carbonel would sit beside her on the
window-ledge making strange cat noises in his throat
until Rosemary went to bed, when he would slip
silently away into the twilight on his own affairs.

On the fourth day after the adventure with the Wishing Magic, John came to fetch Rosemary and they set
off with their sandwiches.

'You know,' said Rosemary as they made their way to the bus stop, 'I have not bothered very much about the cat side of all this before. I have only been thinking of freeing Carbonel because he is such a darling.'

'A pretty crotchetty darling, if you ask me!' said John.

'But don't you see, that is because he is so worried about everything? It must be dreadful for him to see his poor subjects being so badly treated. I shouldn't be surprised if all great exiles were pretty snappy, people like Napoleon and Charles II, I mean; only that is not the sort of thing that gets into history books.'

Carbonel looked round. He had been stalking on ahead. Rosemary had thought him too far away to hear the conversation, but she was mistaken. However, he seemed not displeased at being compared to Napoleon and Charles II.

'I suppose we are wise to go to the market again?' asked Rosemary.

'Well, it does seem to be the sort of place where things happen, doesn't it?' said John.

'I believe we shall find HER there,' said Carbonel. They had brought the broom with them so that he could talk to them. 'As like as not she didn't sell her broom until she had found the place where she wanted to settle. It stands to reason. Besides, catch her wasting money on shoe leather, when the broom would take her for nothing.'

They were later in setting off than before, and the streets were full of busy people. The expedition began badly. The sky was cold and grey so that they had had some difficulty in persuading Mrs Pendlebury Parker to let them go off for the day. There was a queue at the bus stop, and the conductor had a headache. Not that he told anyone about it, but it made him cross, so that when he saw Carbonel slipping up the stairs after the children, he called out:

'Now then, no cats upstairs! What do you think this is, a blinking Noah's Ark?' and to the children's indignation he picked up the outraged Carbonel by the scruff of his neck and dumped him on the pavement. There was no time for John and Rosemary to get off too, and as the bus gathered speed they saw the cat, looking the soul of indignation, left standing on the pavement.

There seemed nothing to do about it, but go on as they had arranged.

'But without Carbonel I almost hope we don't find Mrs Cantrip,' said Rosemary uneasily.

'Well, it doesn't seem very likely that we shall, anyway, so I shouldn't worry,' said John cheerfully. 'We have absolutely no clue to go on. Besides, she is only an ordinary old woman now. You said she'd retired from being a witch.'

Rosemary said nothing. John was a matter-of-fact person and it was hard to describe anything so intangible as feelings to him.

'I tell you what,' said John when they had got off the bus, 'why not say the Summoning Words? After all, it was Carbonel who wanted us to get on with things, so he couldn't mind.'

'I suppose I could. It is serious this time, not showing off.'

'Of course it is serious. Besides, you are his mistress, after all.'

They found a quiet corner between two cars in the

parking places beside the market, and Rosemary shut
her eyes and said the Summoning Words:

> *By squeak of bat*
> *And brown owl's hoot,*
> *By hellebore,*
> *And mandrake root,*
> *Come swift and silent*
> *As the tomb,*
> *Dark minion*
> *Of the twiggy broom.*

When Rosemary opened her eyes again she said, 'I
forgot to ask you. Have you any sandwiches that he will
like? Mine are only ham and hard boiled egg, and I
know he won't like those.'

They tore a corner of John's packet and found that
his were potted meat and jam.

'Look here,' said Rosemary. 'We shall have to put in
some time before Carbonel can possibly get here. Let's
go and buy him a tin of sardines. He will be frightfully
hungry after walking all the way here. I think we can
get a little tin for sevenpence. Let's go to the grocery
stalls.'

They set off walking slowly up and down the market.
They meant quite honestly to be looking for sardines,
but it was all so interesting that it was some time before
they reached the aisle where most of the grocery stalls
were to be found. They bought a little tin of sardines
from a stall which was a jumble of all kinds of
tinned foods which had a large placard over it which
said SMASHING REDUCTIONS! A PENNY OFF THE
SHILLING! So instead of paying sevenpence they
got it for sixpence halfpenny. It was not till they had
wandered to the end of the market that they realized

that there was no key with it with which to open
the tin.

'What a swizzle!' said John. 'Let's go back and ask
for one.'

They went back, but the fat man in charge of the
stall merely said:

'Well, what do you expect for sixpence halfpenny?
P'r'aps you'd like a knife and fork?' and everybody
laughed.

'How cross people are today!' sighed Rosemary.

'A fat lot of use a tin is without an opener,' said John.
'The sight of a tin we can't open will make Carbonel
cross as well, and I shouldn't blame him!'

'I tell you what,' said Rosemary. 'Perhaps the
second-hand man will have one he would let us borrow.' So they went to see.

The old man saw them coming over the heads of
several people. As soon as he caught sight of Rosemary
he waved an imaginary fairy wand, pointed the toe of
a battered boot, and did what he meant to be a fairy
pirouette. Then he wheezed in a way that Rosemary
recognized as a laugh and she laughed too, more because he was such a nice, friendly little man, than
because she thought it funny. The fairy wand business
was becoming a regular joke.

'They still 'aven't come in yet!' he said between
wheezes.

'It isn't a fairy wand we want today, it's a sardine tin
opener,' said Rosemary gravely.

'A sardine tin opener?' he said, going off into a
paroxysm of wheezes. 'You'll be the death of me!' he
said at last, wiping his eyes. But he rummaged about in
an old box and brought out a key, very old and rusty,
but nevertheless a key.

'I don't fancy sardines myself, but it takes all sorts to make a world. If it was sweets, now, it would be different. A regular sweet tooth I've got.'

Rosemary took the opener from him. 'Thank you very much indeed! How much is it?'

'I'll make you a present of it!' said the old man gallantly, and turned away to attend to a customer.

It was precisely this minute that the two children became aware of Carbonel licking his dusty paws a few feet away. Far from being cross at having been summoned, he was most gracious.

'I wondered if you would have enough sense to say the Words,' he said. 'Of course I was coming anyway, but the Words give one's paws the power of coming the shortest way possible. I was following the bus route when they whipped me round and down an alley I had never noticed before. Got me here in half the time. Not a whole tin of sardines specially for me? Really, I feel quite touched! Believe me, I shall never forget it!'

And Carbonel rubbed himself against the children's bare legs, winding in and out between them and purring, as John said, 'Like a space ship.'

They found a couple of packing cases at the edge of the stalls and settled down to eat their sandwiches, while Carbonel, still purring, licked the sardine tin until even the smell of sardine had gone.

'I tell you what I bags we do,' said Rosemary, as she wiped the crumbs from her lap. 'Let's go and buy the old man a present. He has been so jolly kind and helpful. We shouldn't have found either the hat or the cauldron without him, and now there is the opener.'

'That's a good idea. But whatever could we give him?'

'He said he'd got a terribly sweet tooth,' said Rosemary. 'There is a sweet shop over there I went to once. Let's go there and see what we can afford.'

She led the way to the little shop where she had weighed the merits of toffee apples and liquorice boot-laces on the day that she had first met Carbonel. What a long time ago it seemed now! When they reached the shop they were in deep discussion as to what happened to a sweet tooth if you had to have false ones, so that Rosemary did not notice anything different about the shop at first.

'I don't expect they can replace a sweet tooth,' she was saying. 'That is why old people don't seem to like toffee. Besides ...'

John interrupted, 'Is this the shop you mean? What a miserable place!'

It was indeed. There was no longer a cheerful display of jars of sweets, of pink coconut ice, and sticks of pep-permint rock. Except for one or two jars of pallid toffee and some dusty odds and ends of stationery the window was empty. Rosemary looked with distaste at two dead blue-bottles which lay on their backs near some yellow-ing envelopes. 'I think this is it,' she said doubtfully.

'Well, p'r'aps that explains it,' said John. And he pointed to a hand-printed notice which was stuck rather crookedly on to the window with stamp paper:

UNDER NEW MANGEMENT

it said in wobbly capital letters.

'Well, I shouldn't think the "new mangement" gets many customers!'

But as he spoke a young woman with a whimpering small boy opened the door with an angry jangle of the bell and went in. 'I say, look at that!'

Rosemary looked where he pointed excitedly. Over

the door was another notice which said KATIE CAN-
TRIP. LICENSED TO SELL TOBACCO.

John whistled. 'Come on!' he said.

Rosemary began to say, 'Don't go in till we've decided what to do ...' but it was too late. John had
opened the door with a jangle of the bell that could not
be ignored, and Carbonel had slipped in after him.
There was nothing for Rosemary to do but follow down
the two steps into the shop.

19

Mrs Cantrip

I T was dark inside the shop, and the old woman behind
the counter was so busy with her customer that she paid
no attention to the children. She was grinning and bob-
bing, but saying nothing to the young woman, who was
talking very fast and angrily, while she held the small
boy by the arm.

'I tell you straight,' she was saying. 'It's the third
time 'e's 'ad a stomach ache after eating your 'ome
made sweets. Once I could 'ave understood, because 'e
never was a child to know when to stop. But today 'e'd
only sucked a couple, that I do know, when the poor
little kid was doubled up. I'm not one to complain,
neither, but you can take the rest of them back!' And
she threw the bag of sweets on the counter. The little
boy howled anew, as much at the sight of his property
bursting its bag and bouncing all over the floor, as at
the pangs of stomach ache. The young woman gave
him a shake.

'And don't you ever let me find you coming 'ere
again!' she said, and pulled him, still complaining, out
of the shop.

The clanging of the bell died away and the children
watched Mrs Cantrip as she scrabbled round the floor,
picking up the sweets. As she put them back into the jar
without so much as a dust, both John and Rosemary
were doubtful about helping her to pick them up. However, it gave Rosemary a moment or two to notice that
the old woman had made some attempt to tidy herself

since the day she had sold the broom. Her grey hair was twisted into a wispy bun by means of several large hairpins that reminded John of staples. She wore a shawl over her shoulders edged with scarlet bobbles, some of them missing, and a grubby apron with a pattern of enormous pink flowers on it.

She peered short-sightedly over the counter and said to John, amiably enough:

'What can I do for you, lovie?'

There was a pause while the cat and the two children instinctively drew nearer together. It was John who spoke first.

'Are you Mrs Cantrip?' he asked.

'Katie Cantrip, that's me,' said the old woman. 'Licensed to sell tobacco,' she added with some pride.

'Then, if you please, we want you to tell us the Silent Magic that will make Carbonel free for ever.'

The old woman stiffened, and the amiability drained from her face as completely as water drains from a sieve, leaving her sharp nose and chin looking sharper than ever. Her deep-set eyes snapped angrily.

'Have you got that cat there?' she asked harshly.

'I'm here!' said Carbonel, and he leapt up on to the counter.

Mrs Cantrip seemed to pull herself together.

'Well, we'd better talk it over fair and square. Put the broom on the counter so that we can all hear His Highness Prince Carbonel talking.'

Carbonel's tail twitched at the very end where it hung down from the counter, otherwise he might not have noticed the mock deference with which she gave him his full title.

'Do as SHE says,' he said, without taking his great golden eyes off her. 'But don't leave the broom unguarded for an instant. Goodness knows what she might get up to.'

So they put the broom longwise down the counter, with the twigs still wrapped in Rosemary's shoe bag, and John held it one end, and Rosemary held it the other, and from the other side of the counter Mrs Cantrip laid her gnarled hand on the middle. But as she stroked the wooden handle the children felt the broom quiver in response.

'Ah, my beauty!' said the old woman, so softly that Rosemary was startled. 'We had some fine times together, you and me! Do you remember swooping over the North Pole with the Northern Lights flickering through your tail? And beating back home against a north-east gale with the clouds scudding over the moon so thick and dark that many a broom would have lost its way? But not you, my beauty! Ah, you were as fine a besom as ever took the sky, but now you are old, and so am I, and the glory is gone from us.' She stroked the broom and cruddled over it like a woman with a sick child. Rosemary seized on her softened mood. 'But why won't you set Carbonel free?'

At the mention of the cat the softened mood was over.

'Why should I set him free? I always hated him, else why should I have gone to the trouble of binding him with a second Magic?'

'Why do you hate me?' asked Carbonel. His tail was still now, but his eyes never left the old woman's face. 'I worked well for you.'

'Oh, yes, you did your work,' said Mrs Cantrip bitterly, 'but only because you had to. I never tamed your proud spirit. However powerful the magic I made, you were always there with your air of disdain and disapproval as though you were the master and I the servant. And just as much as you withheld your will, my spells were that much short of perfection.'

'Your own pride was responsible for that. If you had been content to have a common cat for your accomplice you would have had your way. But you chose a Royal Cat.'

'That is all over now,' said Rosemary. 'Can't you forget it, and tell us the Silent Magic so that we can set him free?'

'I shall never tell you, you may be sure of that. If you want to know, you must find it out for yourselves. Besides, it is a Silent Magic so no one can say it. It was written down, and I have burnt my books, haven't I?'

'Have you?' asked Carbonel sweetly. 'I doubt if it was only sugar and water that goes into these sweets of yours that give the children such stomach ache!'

John and Rosemary looked at the rows of jars on the shelves behind her, and in each one the sweets glowed very faintly, red and green and yellow, in a way that they had certainly never seen before in a sweet shop.

'Well, what of it?' said Mrs Cantrip sullenly. 'It was only a very little magic I mixed with them to make 'em go farther. It didn't do any real harm. A bit of stomach ache is good for children. Teaches 'em self control.'

Her eyes wavered beneath Carbonel's unwinking stare.

'Then if you are still doing magic, you didn't burn all your books!'

'I did burn them,' said Mrs Cantrip angrily. 'Well, all of them except one,' she admitted.

'Where is it?' said John and Rosemary together.

'That I'll never tell you!' said the old woman

fiercely. But as she spoke the shop door burst open, and half a dozen people came tumbling in. Now the shop was so small that it could only hold four people with comfort, so that when six people squeezed in, in addition to John and Rosemary, and those people angry and gesticulating, there was barely room to move. Above the hubbub a brawny man who seemed to head the company shouted:

'Are you Mrs Cantrip?'

'That's me. I'm Katie Cantrip, licensed to sell tobacco.'

'Well, why don't you sell tobacco instead of this rubbish? 'Ere, this is what you sold me, see!' and he thrust a handful of evil-smelling brown stuff under her long nose.

'So I did!' said the old woman blandly. 'That's tobacco all right. I ought to know, because I grew it myself in my own back yard,' she added with pride.

'You what ...?' roared the man.

'Yes, and what is this rubbish you sold me instead of notepaper!' said a shrill voice behind him. 'Superfine Azure Bond is what I paid for, and nothing but dead leaves when I got home. I'll have the law on you!' But her shrill protests were drowned by further complaints.

'Made my Tommy sick, her sweets did!'

'And my Lucy!'

'It ought not to be allowed!'

'Who does she think she is?'

'Give us our money back, missus!'

Fists were shaken and threats were thick in the air. John said to Mrs Cantrip:

'You had better give them back their money, or I think there will be trouble.'

'How can I? I haven't got any,' said the old woman.

'But if you was to let me have the broom back I could be over their heads in a winking!' she said craftily.

'Oh no you don't!' said Carbonel.

She peered uneasily from side to side at the angry people, and Rosemary felt quite sorry for the old woman.

'We can't give you the broom, but we will help you, won't we?'

John nodded. 'Take her into the room at the back. And Carbonel had better go with you to see fair play. Give me all the money you've got. It's lucky Daddy sent me five shillings this morning. Hurry up!'

Mrs Cantrip ran uncertainly to the end of the counter, hesitated and turned back and went with Rosemary with Carbonel close on her heels. Their disappearance raised a fresh shower of angry cries from the defrauded customers, so to make himself heard John climbed on to a chair.

'Ladies and gentlemen!' he shouted. 'Ladies and gentlemen! If you will jolly well be quiet for a minute, on behalf of Mrs Cantrip, I will give you your money back, if I can,' and turning to the angry man he said, 'What do you want?'

'My tobacco or my money. That's fair, isn't it? I paid three and sixpence for this rubbish!'

Even from where he was standing on the chair John noticed an extraordinary smell coming from the torn packet. He counted out three and sixpence (there was three halfpence in the cash drawer, and a safety pin). This made a very large hole in their total of six and threepence. However, the brawny man seemed satisfied and, muttering something about 'the police next time', elbowed his way out of the shop. With his departure the remaining customers seemed a little less aggressive.

Under the counter was a cardboard box of stationery with the maker's seal still unbroken, so that John was able to replace the notepaper and envelopes from this, feeling pretty certain that it would not turn into dry leaves on the way home, as the other had done. Luckily the sweets had only been sold for a few pence, so that when the last customer came for her money he was only tuppence short. She was a nice, motherly person, and when she saw John's anxious face she said:

'Don't take on, dearie! It doesn't matter about the tuppence, but don't let your Grannie do it again.'

John was so shocked at the idea of Mrs Cantrip being taken for his grandmother, that he quite forgot to say 'Thank you.'

When she had gone he locked the door and hung up the notice that said 'Closed', and heaved a sigh of relief.

In a few minutes he rejoined Rosemary in the little room that opened off the shop. It was surprisingly tidy. There was very little furniture, but what there was was clean and orderly. Rosemary was making a cup of tea.

'It looked all right in the packet,' she said, 'but I don't think we had better drink any. It might turn us into something.'

'Probably something creepy with a lot of legs,' said John. Rosemary shuddered. Mrs Cantrip said nothing, but she took the cup that Rosemary poured out for her and blew on it gustily.

'Well, I got rid of them!' he said, and told them what had happened. 'But I shouldn't open the shop for a day or two until it has blown over,' he said to Mrs Cantrip, who did not even look up from her tea.

'Go away!' she said sourly.

'Well, of all the ungrateful people!' began Rosemary. 'When all we are doing is to try to help you!'

'It's no use!' said Carbonel. 'Sulking, that's what she's doing. Best leave her to get over it.'

'Come on, Rosie,' said John. 'Let's go!'

'All right, I suppose we had better.' She turned to Mrs Cantrip. 'But we shall come back for the Silent Magic, make no mistake about that!'

Mrs Cantrip poured her tea into the saucer and drank it noisily, but still she said nothing. The children found a side door that opened on to an alley which led back to the Market Square.

'Well, I do think she might have said "Thank you", considering it cost us every penny we've got!' said Rosemary indignantly. 'And I think it was awfully brave of you to face all those angry people like that. All the same, I wish we hadn't got to walk back.'

'Oh well, things might be a good deal worse,' said John.

'Look here, I've got something to show you. Where can we go that's quiet and private?'

'What about the Cathedral where we had our sandwiches the other day?'

'Good idea,' said John.

20

The book

THEY set off for the Cathedral, John humming a tune to himself. Rosemary looked at him suspiciously. He seemed to mind remarkably little that they had no money left and had failed in their attempts to get Mrs Cantrip to tell them the Silent Magic.

'You look awfully fat!' she said. 'What have you got inside your coat?'

'Wouldn't you like to know?' said John in an irritating voice.

'Not particularly!' said Rosemary untruthfully.

They walked in silence to the top of the High Street. It was a strain for Rosemary because it was rather a long way and she was bursting with curiosity. The rooks were cawing noisily in the tops of the swaying elm trees, and the fat little angels on either side of the clock were striking three o'clock as they made their way to the same seat as before.

'Now then, do you want to see?' said John. Luckily Carbonel said 'Of course we do!' which relieved Rosemary of the problem of how to say she did, and yet keep her dignity.

'Well,' said John. 'When I had locked the door behind the nice woman, I was just going to follow you when I remembered that before you got Mrs Cantrip to go out of the room, she ran to the end of the counter, as though she was going to do something, and then thought better of it and turned back again. Well, Sherlock Holmes says that in any emergency women always rush to the thing that they value most. It's a first class story, that, it's the one where ...'

'Oh, never mind about Sherlock Holmes!' interrupted Rosemary, her dignity forgotten. 'Do go on!'

'Well,' said John again. He was evidently enjoying himself. 'I went to the end of the counter, and all I could see were three little drawers underneath. One was empty except for a candle-end and a piece of string, the middle one was full of bills, and the third ...'

'Yes?' breathed Rosemary.

John was unbuttoning his jacket. From inside he took out a battered, ancient-looking book. Only one of its powdery leather covers was there, and that hung by a single strand of thread. The pages were thick and yellow, and covered with cramped writing and curious diagrams in red and black ink.

Carbonel was standing with his front paws on John's knee, with his ears pricked and his great eyes intent on the writing.

'Oh, wise young human!' he said. 'Oh, Prince among Boys! Through your wisdom and perspicacity we have found the book of spells with the Silent Magic!'

For one pardonable minute Rosemary wrestled with a feeling of the unfairness of things. After all that she had done for Carbonel the highest praise she had been given was that she 'knew how to stroke'. But it was only for a minute. Even if she had known about Sherlock Holmes she had to admit that she would never have thought of applying what she had read to Mrs Cantrip.

'I think you are the cleverest boy I know!' she said, and she really meant it. John went quite pink at all this praise.

'It wasn't so bad,' he said modestly. But Carbonel

was oblivious of everything but the book. He was trying to turn the pages with his paw.

'Every witch has a book like this. They're handed down from one to another, and each one adds what new spells she has discovered.'

'Like cookery recipes,' said Rosemary.

'This is the right book, sure enough. I'd know it anywhere, though of course SHE would never let me look inside it. Search about half-way through.'

John flipped over the pages at random.

'What is this ... "To ensure the blight on a neighbouring garden. Increase ingredients according to distance away required!" ... hm. That's not it. What's this? "An infallible love potion ..." Oh, who cares about love potions? Here, what is this? "A Silent Magic for the Use of ..." Hi, Carbonel, look what you've done!'

As John began to read this last title the cat had said 'Hush!' and in a desperate effort to cover the words with his paws had knocked the precious book off John's knees on to the pavement.

'Whatever did you do that for?' asked John crossly.

'Don't you see?' said Carbonel. 'It is a Silent Magic, and if you say it aloud it is broken and spoilt!'

They picked up the book and dusted it carefully. It seemed none the worse. But nobody noticed that something had fallen from between the pages. They found the place again with some difficulty, and craning over John's shoulder this is what Rosemary read:

'SHE WHO WOULD UNDO A BINDING MAGIC must take the plait of Binding Plants which was twisted when the Magic was first made. This will probably be Dry as Tinder but no matter. Fill the Cauldron with Seven Pipkins of Puddle Water. When the water comes to the boil she must drop in the Plait of Weeds without delay and ride widdershins seven times round the Boiling Pot. This done, she must take the Binding Plants from the cauldron (these will now be found green and lush), and must untwist the Plait, being sure that she make no sound or complaint, though they tear her fingers. With the unbinding of the weeds the One bound will for ever be made free. The following words must be said Silently as the Plait is Unwound ...'

'Yes, but look here,' said John. 'Where on earth is this wretched plait?'

The three looked at each other blankly. For a minute they none of them said anything, but their thoughts were very much the same. It was too bad when the final piece of the puzzle seemed to be falling into place to find that, after all, they were as far as ever from completing it.

At last Rosemary spoke. 'We don't seem to be any nearer the end than before,' she said gloomily.

They sat in a row on the seat staring before them at the brilliant green of the grass, at the flagged path with here and there a fallen leaf, and at the sparrows that hopped with maddening cheerfulness round their feet. But they were none of them aware of what they were looking at. Rosemary, with her mind intent on where to find a seven-year-old plait of withered creepers, idly watched an old man in a green apron sweeping up the leaves and bits of paper that untidy people had dropped on the path. Somewhere near he had a bonfire; she could tell by the smell. He swept the rubbish into a little pile by the seat, and just as he bent down to load it into his wheelbarrow by scooping it up with two bits of board, she jumped up and pounced on the pile.

'Oh, please don't sweep it up!' she said desperately. 'You have got something valuable of ours here. I'm sure I saw you sweep it up!'

To the astonishment of John, Carbonel, and the old man, she began scrabbling frantically among the leaves and bits of paper and bus tickets. Suddenly she made a pounce.

'I've got it!' she said, and rose triumphantly to her feet. John was staring at her with his mouth open, and even Carbonel looked surprised.

'Is she all right in the head?' asked the gardener.

'Of course I am!' said Rosemary indignantly. 'I say, I am awfully sorry I have messed up your path again, but I will sweep it up for you if you will lend me your broom.'

But, muttering that 'he didn't know what children were coming to!' the old man collected the rubbish together once more and trundled it away in his barrow, still muttering darkly to himself. Rosemary was too excited to notice what he did.

'I've got it! I've got it!' she said. 'I remember that something fell out of the book when we dropped it. I thought vaguely it was a piece of paper, but I was so anxious to see the spell I never thought any more about it; and just as I was watching the rubbish being swept up, I suddenly thought what it must have been. Why, in a minute or two it would have been on the bonfire! Look here!'

In the palm of her hand lay a coil of roughly plaited twigs, dry and brittle as tinder. There was still a withered leaf attached to one of the strands, which might once have been ivy.

'Mrs Cantrip must have pressed it in her magic book, like Mummy pressed a sweet pea from her wedding bouquet in her Bible ...' They turned over the thick pages of the book, and sure enough, between two plain pages at the end was a depression into which the plait exactly fitted.

'You're a wonder!' said John. But Carbonel's heart was so full that all he could do was to rub himself against Rosemary's legs and purr and purr and purr. There was no need to say anything. It was her turn to go pink with pleasure.

'There is only the hat to get now,' said Rosemary, 'and that will be easy.'

'I left the Players' handbill in my other jacket pocket, but I'll look it up the minute we get home,' said John.

'In two days' time the moon will be full, and that will mean the next Lawgiving,' said Carbonel. 'If only I could be free by then, what bloodshed could I spare my people!'

'Well, we'll have a good try to get the hat tomorrow somehow,' said John. 'But look here, my jolly boys, as I used up every halfpenny we had between us on that ungrateful old Cantrip, we shall have to hoof it home.'

'I tell you what,' said Rosemary. 'I feel I could hoof it much better with some tea inside me. Let's go and see Miss Maggie at the Copper Kettle.'

'Far be it from me to deny you your simple pleasures,' said Carbonel, 'but my mind is on higher matters than cream buns and lemonade. I have other things to do. Guard the book well!' And with tail erect and head held high he padded purposefully away.

21

More plans

JOHN and Rosemary ate an enormous tea. I shall not bother you with details of what they had because if you think of all the things to eat that you like best you will know all about it without being told. Miss Maggie and her sister were delighted to see them. It was rather a relief to talk about ordinary things, such as the difficulty of finding someone really reliable to wash up, and how many of the Women's Instituters had come again and brought their friends, and how their brother had been so deeply impressed by the numbers of their customers. It was only when Miss Maggie said that she would so much like to write a little note of thanks to the kind person who had lent them all the beautiful china that Rosemary jumped up hurriedly.

'Goodness! It's half past five, and we promised to be home by six! We simply must go. Thank you for the wonderful tea!'

With the book safely buttoned inside John's coat, and a good tea inside them, the children hardly noticed the walk home. The car was standing outside number ten when they reached Tottenham Grove. They ran upstairs, still discussing plans for getting the hat next day. Jeffries was drinking a cup of tea.

'Hallo, dears!' said Mrs Brown. 'Had a happy day?'

'Lovely!' said both John and Rosemary.

'I'm so glad. You know, Mrs Pendlebury Parker really is extremely kind. What do you think? There is a

Garden Fête tomorrow at Walsingham Court, and you two are to go, and as Mrs Parker has a committee that afternoon, she has asked me if I would mind taking you instead. The sewing is nearly done. You would like to go, wouldn't you?'

Rosemary pulled herself valiantly together. At any other time she would have loved it.

'I expect I shall enjoy it no end ... when I get there. And it's lovely that you are going to have a day off. It's only that John and me had planned something else.'

John made no attempt to hide his disgust. 'It will mean clean nails and a tie!' he said tragically. But Jeffries broke into his lamentations.

'I'll stand you a go at the coconut shy, but not if you don't look slippy now. We must be pushing off, ma'am. Thank you for the tea.'

Rosemary watched the car as it drove away, and then she went slowly upstairs. What a lot had happened since the day school had broken up and she had bounced her satchel up the stairs. Full moon in two days! If only they could have got out of going to the fête next day! But she could think of no way that would not seem both rude and ungrateful. It was really very kind of Mrs Pendlebury Parker, and her mother, she knew, would thoroughly enjoy the change from sides to middling. There was clearly nothing to be done, except to enjoy the fête as much as possible, she thought guiltily.

Half-way through supper they heard the faint tinkle of the telephone that stood in the hall, and Mrs Walker came half-way up the stairs and called up.

'It's for Rosie!' she said sourly. 'As if I haven't enough to do, and my feet are killing me.'

Rosemary ran downstairs.

'It's me, John,' said the small tinny voice the other end. 'It's all right. What do you think? The Netherley Players are acting at the fête! Jeffries is coming to fetch you and your mother at 2.30, so bring the Broom and the Cauldron and Carbonel with you.'

'Yes, but John ...'

'Can't stop now. See you tomorrow.' And Rosemary found herself protesting to a dead receiver.

After supper she discussed it with Carbonel. He had just come upstairs from the basement.

'Phoo! You do smell of bloaters!' said Rosemary.

'Bloaters? So that is what they were,' said the cat, licking his shirt front complacently. 'Delicious. Now, you say that these play actors with the hat will be at this place tomorrow? It seems to me it will be next to impossible to get them to give you the Hat, but they might be persuaded to lend it to you for half an hour. John is quite right. The obvious thing for you to do is to take Cauldron, Broom, and me with you.'

'That's all very well!' said Rosemary, 'but Mummy and Jeffries will never let me. If they see me taking cats and coal-scuttles to a garden fête they'll think I've gone mad!'

'Well, don't let them see you. Really, Rosemary, you have no ingenuity.'

A number of rather angry replies came into Rosemary's mind at this, but she remembered Napoleon and Charles the Second and swallowed the retorts that came to her lips.

'You can surely smuggle us into the back of the car somehow,' said Carbonel coolly.

'After all,' thought Rosemary, 'it isn't being naughty, only odd, to take them with me.' And she went on aloud: 'All right, but you will have to go inside the cauldron. Either that or I shall have to leave you behind and say the Summoning Words when we get there.'

Carbonel opened his mouth to say something indignant, but when she pointed out what a long way it was, he changed his mind.

'Very well,' he said with dignity. 'I will travel in the cauldron, but have the goodness to clean out the remains of the Rainbow Magic. Even SHE used to wash up properly afterwards.'

It was no use, thought Rosemary. He always had the last word.

'Dear Carbonel!' She laughed and, greatly daring, kissed him on the top of his sleek black head. He did not seem displeased.

Mrs Brown did not have to go to Tussocks next morning, and during a delightfully leisurely lunch Rosemary said:

'Mummy, wouldn't it be a good idea to take the old rug off the foot of my bed this afternoon, so that we could sit on the grass even if it is damp? We don't want to catch cold, do we?' she added virtuously. Her mother laughed.

'I've never known you bother about whether the grass is damp or not before. But it would be a good idea, all the same.'

'Well, it wouldn't do to use Mrs Parker's beautiful fur car rug, would it?' said Rosemary.

Rosemary was ready a good hour before the car was due to fetch them. She was wearing her best summer frock with blue smocking on the front and two blue hair ribbons. She had cleaned out the cauldron. The remains of the wishing spell did smell rather nasty, and she had black-leaded its sides and polished the copper band. She felt that it ought to be looking its best, as this was its final magic, and somehow she knew that the battered old thing was grateful. She even contemplated tying a red hair ribbon on the handle of the broom, but decided against it because John would undoubtedly laugh at her. Finally she oiled the handles of the cauldron so that they should make as little noise as possible when she smuggled everything down. Even Carbonel had to admit that she had made a good job of it.

When at last it was time to expect Jeffries with the car, everything was ready. Just as she heard the distant ring of the front doorbell her mother called out:

'What are you doing, Rosie?'

'I've just made a cup of tea for you and Jeffries, a sort of stirrup cup,' she said. And without waiting for a reply she ran downstairs with Carbonel in the cauldron covered with the old rug, and the broom under her arm. She did not run far, because it was so heavy, but she got safely to the hall at last. She placed the precious things so that when she opened the door they would be out of sight behind it, and then she flung the door back. There was John on the doorstep – an unfamiliar John with neatly brushed hair, socks, and a long-sleeved shirt with a tie.

'What an age you have been,' he said. 'I thought you were never coming. What are you pulling faces for?' he began. Rosemary interrupted hurriedly.

'I promised Mrs Walker that I would open the door because of her poor feet, you know.' And turning to Jeffries she said, 'Would you like a cup of tea? I've just made one for you.'

'But we've only just finished dinner,' said John, who seemed determined to make things as difficult as possible.

143

'Not you, silly! Mr Jeffries. It's all ready up-stairs.'

'Very kind of you, I'm sure,' said the chauffeur. 'I can always do with a cuppa.'

Rosemary waited until his gleaming leggings had disappeared up the first flight of stairs; then she said to John, who was looking extremely puzzled:

'You are stupid! I only did that so that we could get the things in the car without being seen.' And she closed the door.

'All right, keep your hair on!' said John cheerfully. 'How was I to know that?'

'I didn't mean to be cross, but it was horrid when Jeffries thought I was being kind, and really I only wanted to get him out of the way, like Mummy thinking I was being thoughtful when I suggested taking the rug to cover the things.'

Rosemary moved the door so that they could see the cauldron behind it. Carbonel poked a ruffled head out from under the rug and said crossly:

'I do not like being referred to as "Things"!' and disappeared suddenly as they thought they heard Mrs Walker coming up from the basement.

The children put the cauldron on the floor in the back of the car, with the broom beside it, and the rug arranged carefully on top.

'It doesn't show too much,' said John.

'Have you got the book?' asked Rosemary anxiously. He nodded.

'About the only advantage of this silly get-up is that there is more room to hide things.'

'To think we have got everything except the Hat!' said Rosemary happily.

There was no time to discuss things any further, because just at that moment Jeffries opened the door of the car for Mrs Brown to get into the front seat.

'Are you all right there?' said the chauffeur. The two children nodded. He pressed the starter, and they were off to Walsingham Court.

22

The fête

WALSINGHAM COURT was one of the show places of the neighbourhood. The gardens where the fête was held were magnificent. I am not going to describe them to you, any more than I am going to describe the fête, because if you think of the most beautiful rose gardens and yew walks, and rock gardens and herbaceous borders and orangeries that you have ever seen, you will know exactly what it was like. Just as you will know what the fête was like, with stalls and hoop-las, and tombolas and raffles, and Punch and Judy shows and fortune-tellers. It was hot and sunny, and the children and Mrs Brown wandered round enjoying every bit of it. They spent all their money within the first half-hour, but it did not seem to matter, because there was so much to look at.

Presently Mrs Brown said:

'I simply must sit down! I think I shall watch the dancing display from a deck chair. Would you two like to go off on your own?'

This was the moment they had been waiting for. Rosemary nodded.

'All right, dears. But be back by quarter to four because we have got tickets for the first tea.'

There was no time to reply, because the enclosure reserved for the dancers had already been invaded by a dozen little girls in very pink crinolines and poke bonnets. They were apparently showing their unwillingness to go walking with an equal number of little girls dressed as boys.

'And I don't blame them,' said John. 'Why can't they just say, "Not likely!" or something, instead of this silly dumb crambo business? Come on. I saw where the Netherley Players are doing their stuff.'

Secretly Rosemary would like to have watched the dancing, but she knew that they had a great deal to do and not much time in which to do it. There was a series of notices which pointed the way to the Netherley Players. It seemed that they were giving three performances. The one at two-thirty was over and the next was at five, with a final one at seven. The arrows led to a green, grassy amphitheatre which sloped gently down to a broad paved terrace, behind which was a mass of flowering shrubs and trees.

'What a lovely place for acting!' said Rosemary. 'And look, there is a summer-house over there. I expect that is where they change their clothes. Let's go and see.'

They made their way down the aisle between the rows of empty chairs towards the summer-house. It was a wooden building with two low storeys and a thatched roof. Both children silently thought that it would be first-rate for playing in. When they reached the three shallow steps which led to the door, they became aware that someone was arguing inside.

'I told you it was ridiculous to agree to do two plays,' said a girl's voice crossly.

'And I told you that we should not have got the engagement if we hadn't. Lady Soffit was sure that the same people would come twice if the second performance was something different,' said a man's voice. A third person said something that they could not hear and the man replied:

'Well, now we've got to. The tickets and bills are

all distributed. We *must* put on the Dream at five o'clock, if we have to do it in flannel bags. I know you didn't mean to leave half the tunics behind, but can't you make some more? You have got an hour and a half. There are those old curtains in the van you could cut up. I suppose you didn't leave the sewing machine behind as well?'

'Don't rub it in, Bill. I am most terribly sorry. Of course I haven't left the sewing machine behind. I'll try. But I don't see how I can do it all in time single-handed,' said the girl's voice.

'Good heavens!' replied the man. 'Surely, with three women in the company, you can turn out something?'

'You know quite well that Megs and Sara are completely ham-handed,' said the first voice. 'Nobody would dare to sit down in anything they had made!'

John and Rosemary on the step outside suddenly realized that they were eavesdropping, so John knocked on the door, which swung open as he did so. A man stood with his back to them, but hearing the knock he turned. It was the Occupier. His hair was standing on end as though he had just been running his hands through it, and he said ungraciously:

'What do you want?'

'It's us, sir!' said John.

'Who on earth is "Us"? Good heavens, if it isn't the Lathero twins! Now run away, there's good children. We're in a frightful jam. We've left half the clothes behind. There isn't time to fetch them, and these useless women don't seem capable of making any more in time!' And he ran his fingers through his hair again so that it looked even wilder than before.

'I know. We heard. We didn't mean to listen, but you

were talking so loudly that we couldn't help it,' said John. But Rosemary interrupted.

'Well, I know who could make them for you if any-one could, and that is my mother. She is a real dress-maker.'

'Well, that is not much use to us,' said the Occupier irritably.

'Don't be cross with them, Bill,' said the girl. It was their friend Molly. 'Where is your mother, dear? Do you think we could possibly persuade her to help us? I feel so desperate that I could brave asking anybody!'

'She is watching the dancing display. I'm sure she would help,' said Rosemary. 'Let's go and ask her.'

She and Molly went off together in the direction of the sound of the tinny piano, and John was left standing awkwardly with the actors. Three men who had been sitting disconsolately on a couple of dress baskets, got up and sauntered off, and the two girls who were presum-ably the ham-handed Megs and Sara went on sorting clothes in the corner.

John followed the Occupier on to the little porch, where they both looked anxiously after Molly and Rose-mary.

'I say,' said John. 'You have still got the witch's hat, haven't you?'

'Good heavens!' said the Occupier, whose name was really Bill. 'You're not going to start that again, are you?'

'You did say we could have it, you know,' said John desperately, 'when we had collected everything else for the Magic, and we have. Everything. The broom, the cauldron, the book of spells, and a high old time we had getting them, I can tell you!'

There was an awkward silence, during which Bill lit a cigarette. They were both relieved when Molly and Rosemary arrived accompanied by Mrs Brown.

Molly was talking volubly, and Rosemary was grinning from ear to ear, and her mother was saying 'I see', and 'I think I could'.

'It's all right!' called Rosemary. 'Mummy is going to help! I knew she would,' she added confidently. 'Now you won't have to worry.'

The Occupier shook Mrs Brown warmly by the hand. 'My dear Mrs Lathero ...'

'Brown!' whispered John hurriedly.

'... Mrs Brown. I can't thank you enough ...'

'Thank me when we have got it done,' smiled Mrs Brown. 'We shall need every minute we can get.' Then, turning to Molly, 'Perhaps it would be quicker if I could cut out the clothes on the people who are going to wear them. We needn't bother about such refinements as hems.'

'What can I do?' asked the Occupier humbly.

'Go away and leave us alone,' said Molly firmly. 'Your clothes were not left behind, thank goodness, so we shan't need you. We have exactly one hour and twenty minutes in which to do it all in! Come on Megs, fetch Harry and Adrian to be fitted. Sara, help us to carry these things upstairs to the upper floor. We had better do it up there.'

Rosemary nudged John. 'Have you asked him?' she whispered. But the Occupier's sharp ears heard her.

'What persistent youngsters you are! Yes, he has asked me.'

'Look here, sir,' said John. 'We know that you bought the hat, and that it is a jolly rare thing. We don't expect you to give it us. But won't you lend it just for half an hour, so that we can do the spell now? Then we would never bother you again.'

They waited breathlessly. The young man blew out a cloud of smoke; then he stubbed out his cigarette.

'All right,' he said at last. 'You win. I'll lend you the hat for half an hour, but you must let me come with you to see fair play. I shan't be needed here for a bit, so let's go and fetch it. It isn't being used today, so it is in the property van behind the greenhouses. Lead on, my young Witch of Endor!'

'Right,' said John. 'You go with him and get the hat, Rosie, and I'll go to the car and fetch the things. Meet you behind the glasshouses as soon as I can.'

'What things?' asked Bill.

This was better, thought Rosemary, and, tucking her hand in his arm, she told him the whole story: how they had searched for the cauldron, about the Wishing Magic and the china, and how they had found the Book of Spells and so nearly lost the withered plait of creepers. She had only just finished by the time they had reached the van. The young man disappeared inside it. Presently he called down, 'Catch!' Rosemary held out her arms and something black and furry landed in them. It was the Hat at last!

'The moths have had a regular banquet off some of it,' he said cheerfully as he jumped down again. 'Pretty indigestible, I should think, witch's hat. Hallo, here is John!' Coming down the path was John with the cauldron in one hand and the broom in the other, and Carbonel trotting sedately beside him. When the cat saw the dilapidated Hat he gave a little 'Purrup!'

'Well,' said Bill, 'he is certainly a splendid animal. But I can't hear him talking.' And he laughed in a bless-your-little-fancies way.

'That is because you aren't holding the broom-stick. Here you are, sir,' said John, and he pushed the wooden handle towards the young man so that he, too, could hold it.

'Do him good,' said Carbonel. 'Too cocky by far, he is.'

The Occupier started violently.

'Do you know, I really did think I heard the cat speak!' he said.

'I did,' said Carbonel drily. 'I said, you are too cocky by far.'

'Good heavens!'

'It is a bit upsetting at first,' said Rosemary kindly, 'but you soon get used to it. I dare say it is harder for you, being grown-up, I mean.'

'Well, we aren't here to make polite conversation,' said Carbonel. 'I noticed a small enclosure behind that asparagus bed, with a bonfire burning there already, and no one about. Follow me.'

They all followed, the Occupier, as though in a dream, clutching the broom, and unable to take his eyes off the black cat.

The enclosure was made by a privet hedge which hid a small tool shed, a heap of grass cuttings, and a small, smouldering bonfire.

Rosemary removed the precious withered plait from between the pages of the book of spells. Then she propped the book up against a wheelbarrow.

'You can read it if you like,' she said to the young man. 'But not aloud, because it is a Silent Magic.'

With a dazed expression he turned his fascinated eyes from Carbonel.

'I say, what about a pipkin?' said Rosemary. 'It says "fill the cauldron with seven pipkins of puddle water".'

'What is a pipkin?' asked John.

'A small earthenware jar,' said Carbonel. 'A flower pot with the hole stopped up will do. Rosemary, you can see to that, while someone else gets the fire going.' He turned to the dazed young man. 'That may as well be your job.'

'Yes, yes, of course!' said the Occupier, and at once feverishly began to collect twigs and sticks which he pushed into the smouldering fire, while John got down on his knees and blew on the embers. Rosemary rolled up her handkerchief and pushed it into the hole at the bottom of a flower pot. It took rather a long time to find enough puddle water to fill the flower pot seven times, but by then the fire had been coaxed into blazing quite merrily. At last the three legs of the cauldron were supported above the flames on two large stones and an old brick, and Rosemary put on the Hat. It was much too big, and only by bending her ears down could she keep it up at all. They removed the shoe-bag from the end of the broom. In spite of their care a number of twigs had fallen off inside the bag. In silence they knelt in a ring, waiting for the cauldron to boil. The sounds of the fête drifted in to them, very faint and far away. A great bumble bee buzzed heavily by, intent on his own business, and a thrush was tapping a snail shell insistently on the brick path outside the enclosure. Then the water began to bubble. Rosemary took a deep breath.

'Stand back!' said Carbonel to the others. 'And remember, if you love me, do not make a sound. Rosemary, whatever happens, I implore you not to cry out!'

She nodded. The young man sat down heavily on the wheelbarrow. Rosemary straddled the broom. Although her mouth had been dry with nervousness before, now she was wearing the Hat she felt quite calm and mistress of the situation. The broom quivered expectantly beneath her, and she patted it softly.

'Now!' said Carbonel, and she leant over and dropped the plait into the centre of the swirling water, which rose up to meet it in a froth of winking bubbles. Without thinking twice she said aloud:

> *While the mixture's boiling hot,*
> *Bear me round the reeking pot.*
> *Widdershins, please fly designedly,*
> *Seven times round. And thank you kindly.*

The broom shook itself and rose slowly from the ground. At the same time a swirl of steam rose from the cauldron, so that she only caught glimpses of her friends below as she whirled round; John and the Occupier on the wheelbarrow and gazing upwards open-mouthed, and Carbonel sitting tense and upright on an upturned bucket. The broom was making wide circles at some speed, so that Rosemary's pigtails flew out from beneath the witch's hat, and what with keeping her balance and stopping the hat from slipping over her face like an extinguisher, she had her work cut out.

At the fifth time round, the steam from the cauldron began to sink, by the sixth it had become a mere trickle, and when the broom deposited her gently by the fire after the seventh circle there was no steam at all. Although the fire still burned brightly, the water in the cauldron was placid and still. Rosemary looked eagerly at its unmoving surface, and there, breaking the reflection of her own face, floated a garland made of seven different climbing plants. Very gingerly Rosemary bent over, and with the handle of the broom hooked it out, and lo and behold, there were flowers of wild rose and bryony. There were white trumpets of bindweed,

... and with the handle of the broom hooked it out.

delicately touched with pink, sweet-smelling clusters of honeysuckle, and little purple vetch, and the leaves and tendrils were as green and delicate as the day on which they were picked seven years ago.

As Rosemary knelt down with the garland on her lap, there fell a silence that seemed as though everything was listening, the sounds of the fête died away, the birds stopped their twittering, even the thrush stopped hammering his snail shell and stood motionless with his head on one side. Very carefully, very carefully, so that not one strand of the garland should break, Rosemary began to unravel the plait. And while she unravelled, quite silently in her head she said the spell that she had learnt by heart. (If you do not know how she could say it silently, remember the times you have repeated your homework to yourself quite clearly, without making a sound.) The vetch twined its pale green tendrils round her fingers as though to hinder her, the juice from the crushed berries of the bittersweet made the strands slip from between her feverish fingers, but she went on. And this is the spell she said:

> *Fingle fange, warp and wind,*
> *Weeds that strangle, climb, and bind,*
> *Plants that trip unwary feet,*
> *Bramble, vetch, and bittersweet.*

The scent from the honeysuckle rose sweet and sickly, and so strong that her head began to swim and she felt faint and drowsy, and when she shook off the drowsiness the thorns tore her fingers, but she closed her lips tightly so that no sound should escape, and went on untwisting, untwining.

> *Fangle, fingle, mickle muckle,*
> *Bindweed, ivy, honeysuckle,*

THE FÊTE

Climbing bramble, tendrilled vine,
Loose your hold, untwist, untwine
Silently, without a sound
Free the Slave and loose the Bound.

The scent from the honeysuckle was so strong that only
by a tremendous effort was Rosemary able to finish.
But with the last word of the spell the last twist unravelled itself beneath her torn and bleeding fingers,
and fell to the ground. For a minute the seven strands
lay there, strong and green in the sunlight, and then
beneath her eyes they wilted and shrank, the flowers
dropped their shrivelled petals and the leaves became
dull, the glossy green gave way to dusty brown. And as
a balloon withers and shrinks when the air escapes, so
the strand of creepers diminished and shrank. And when
Rosemary bent down to pick up the withered twig that
had once been honeysuckle, it fell to powder between
her fingers. A little breeze sprang up, and it was scat-
tered and gone.

The fire was nearly out. The cauldron had boiled dry,
and in the bottom was a hole the size of her fist. Rosemary gave a great sigh. She was aware that the thrush
was once more tapping with his snail shell. The noise of
the fête sounded cheerfully on the breeze again. She
stood up with the broom in her hand. Carbonel was still
sitting on the far side of the enclosure.

'Say the Summoning Words!' he said harshly. 'If I
am still bound I must come to you.'

Rosemary said them rather faintly. She felt strangely
tired.

By squeak of bat
And brown owl's hoot,
By hellebore,
And mandrake root,

Come swift and silent
As the tomb,
Dark minion
Of the twiggy broom.

Nothing happened. Carbonel still sat unmoved upon
the bucket. There was a long, long pause. Then very
deliberately he stepped down and came towards her.

'Little mistress!' he said.

'You never called me that before, and now I'm no
longer your mistress,' said Rosemary, and her eyes filled
with tears. 'You didn't have to come this time when I
summoned you!' Carbonel was purring deeply.

'I came in gratitude. That will be a stronger bond
than any spell.' And his warm tongue licked her
scratched hands.

There was a movement on the other side of the enclosure. The young man got up from the wheelbarrow.
He yawned and stretched.

'Extraordinary thing,' he said cheerfully. 'I must
have dropped off to sleep, sitting here bolt upright! I
had a pretty rum dream, too. I'll tell you about it some-
time.'

Rosemary looked inquiringly at Carbonel, who shook
his head.

'It is just as well he should think he dreamt it. It will
save awkward questions.' But only Rosemary heard
him, because only she had the broom.

'It has been a warm day,' she said. 'Thank you very
much for the Hat. We shan't need it any more.'

'Not at all. I hope you had a good game with it. I
say, it's five o'clock! I must fly. Look here, will you and
young John put it back in the van? I will give you the
key, then you can bring it back to the summer-house

when you have locked it up. Here you are. See you later!'

The children listened in silence to his receding foot-steps. Then Rosemary said: 'I know what I am going to do.'

She removed the cauldron, and bent down and blew up the fire again, and then she took the Book of Spells and poked it deep into the smouldering heart of the ashes.

'Stand back!' warned Carbonel, and she jumped away just in time. With a swish, a green flame edged with purple shot up ten feet into the air. For a moment it flashed and flickered, then it wavered and sank. There was nothing to be seen of the book in the bonfire, nothing but a trickle of sluggish, oily-looking smoke.

'You are wise, little mistress!' said Carbonel.

'Well, I think it was just silly of her,' said John. 'Think what fun we could have had with it on wet days.'

'Nothing but evil ever came of that book.'

In silence they put away the flower pot in the tool-shed, then, taking the Broom and the Cauldron with them, they went to replace the Hat in the van.

'Before you put the Broom in the car, I shall say good-bye,' said Carbonel gravely.

'But shan't we see you again ever any more? Must you go?' asked Rosemary.

'I must go. I have work to do. I shall never forget what you and John have done. You will see me at the Full Moon!' he said. He gave Rosemary's hand a little lick, then he turned, and they watched him grow smaller and smaller as he trotted with head and tail erect down a long path bordered on either side with tiger-lilies. Then he turned a corner and was gone.

'How simply beastly,' said John. 'Everything is over

now. We've even missed tea. I'm starving.' Silently he passed Rosemary his handkerchief.

'We ought to feel as pleased as anything, because we have done what we set out to do. But I don't feel as though I shall ever be pleased again.' She blew her nose very hard.

They left the cauldron and the broom in the car suitably hidden under the rug, and then they returned to the summer-house. But it was not possible to feel miserable there for long. To John's relief there was tea, which they ate sitting on the steps. Mrs Brown and Molly, and even Megs and Sara, were still sewing between mouthfuls. The Occupier and the other men teased the children in a friendly sort of way. It was all very jolly and cheerful, and by the time they had started on the second plate of cakes, they felt they knew everyone quite well. The last tunic was nearly done, and Rosemary could see by her mother's smiling face that she was enjoying herself.

'I must admit,' she said to her daughter later, 'that my heart sank when I thought I had got to sew this afternoon, just when I was off for a holiday. But it has been such fun sewing unusual sorts of clothes, and everyone is so friendly that it has not seemed like work at all.'

'Your mother is a wonder,' said the Occupier, and Rosemary flushed with pride. 'I gather from Molly that not only can she work at twice everybody else's speed, but that by some mystic process of hers called "cutting on the cross" she has transformed Oberon's sleeves.'

'And saved yards of stuff into the bargain,' said Molly.

The children and Mrs Brown, as guests of honour, sat in the front row for the next performance. They were acting the fairy part of *A Midsummer Night's*

Dream, and even John, who usually thought of Shakespeare as somebody invented by masters to harass school-boys, admitted that it was 'smashing'. They were transported by the fairy part, and they laughed and laughed at Bottom and his friends. When it was all over the Occupier took them all round the fête again, and John won two coconuts and Rosemary a china kitten in a boot which she decided to give to Mrs Walker. And when it was time at last to meet Jeffries and the car, they were both so tired they could hardly keep their eyes open.

'What a day!' said John, as he and Rosemary flopped into the back seat.

'Did you enjoy it, dears?' asked Mrs Brown.

'We shall never have such a day again!' said Rosemary. 'I wonder what Carbonel meant when he said he would see us at the full moon?' she whispered to John.

'I don't suppose we shall know till tomorrow,' he whispered back.

23

The full moon

THE next day Rosemary was looking pale.

'Too much excitement,' said Mrs Brown. 'I wonder if perhaps you had better stay at home today, instead of coming with me to Tussocks?'

'Oh, Mummy, please!' begged Rosemary. 'If you have nearly finished the sewing I shall hardly have any more time to play with John, and I have got such heaps to talk to him about. Besides, I think I ought to say "Thank you" to Mrs Pendlebury Parker, don't you?'

Her mother smiled. 'Very well, Poppet. But it must be a really early bed for you tonight!'

Although Rosemary felt there was so much she wanted to talk over with John, when she reached Tussocks she found that by common consent they both avoided any reference to Carbonel or Mrs Cantrip, or anything magic at all. They played good, solid games like Cowboys and Indians all morning, and in the afternoon they built a tree house, which was fun, until Mrs Pendlebury Parker decided that it was not safe and made them take it down again.

When Rosemary and her mother reached home in the evening, Mrs Brown said, firmly:

'Now, we will have supper straight away; scrambled eggs and jam tart, and then you can have your bath and hop into bed. You may take a book with you if you like.'

Rosemary had her bath in the usual bower of other people's drying stockings, then she chose *The Wind in the*

Willows, kissed her mother good night and got into bed. But she could not read. She sat propped against the pillows with the book open before her, but her mind was not on the adventures of Toad and Mole and Rat. It would keep going over the events of the past three weeks. What fun it had all been. What would become of Mrs Cantrip? How would Carbonel win back his place at the head of his kingdom? She closed her eyes to think the better, but she must have fallen asleep, for when she opened them again it was dusk, and the book had slipped to the floor. Something dark and furry leapt on to her bed, and licked her cheek with a familiar rough tongue. She was wide awake at once.

'Carbonel! I did so hope you would come! What are you going to do? Is it the Law Giving tonight?'

Carbonel was kneading the blanket with his front paws and purring rhythmically. 'Oh, wait a minute while I fetch the broom!' She jumped out of bed and ran to the wardrobe. 'Now then!'

'It is, as you say, the Law Giving tonight. Would you like to come?'

'Oh, may I? How lovely! Where is it? And how? And what about John? He would be terribly disappointed if he missed it!'

'Patience, Rosemary. As to where, it will be on the roof of the Town Hall, where it has been at every full moon for four hundred years. And how? By Broom. The fact that the moon is full tonight will give it temporary life, and by Broom we will fetch John from Tussocks. But we must wait for the moon to rise. In the meantime you had better be composing instructions, and mind they are accurate,' he went on in his old manner. 'You can't afford to make mistakes when you are flying high.'

Rosemary put on her old red dressing gown and her slippers with the bobbles on them; then she knelt on the chair by the window, with Carbonel on the sill beside her. The sky was darkening, and the vista of roofs stretched dim and shadowy, away into the distance. Down below she could see countless moving shapes.

'Carbonel, look! Running along the top of the wall ... hundreds of cats!'

'My people!' he said. 'This is a night they will never forget. As yet they know nothing of my return. I thought it best to descend on an unsuspecting enemy. Only Malkin, my father's friend and adviser, has seen me. He is an old, old animal.'

'But I have never seen so many cats! Look at them! All running along the garden wall!'

There was a steady stream of animals, black, white, grey, and tabby, silently but purposefully trotting along the garden wall in the same direction, continually joined by other cats where other walls intersected.

'This is one of the main roads from the outlying parts,' said Carbonel.

The sky behind the roof-tops was becoming lighter.

'Look!' said Carbonel. 'The moon!'

As he spoke, a tiny segment of silver rose from a bank of clouds low on the horizon. Rosemary's hand lay on the cat's sleek back, and she felt him stiffen. He was making low, crooning, cat noises in his throat. As the moon rose majestically in sight – a superb moon, round as a pumpkin and golden as honey, filling the roof-top world with light, and deep, mysterious shadow, Carbonel rose to his feet, lifted his head and sniffed the air, and the crooning noise turned to a bubbling wail, which rose and fell, and rose again to a wild, high note which struck the ear like a trumpet call. Then it sank once again to silence. When the moon was sailing high above the cloud rack, he spoke.

'To Broom, Rosemary!'

And Rosemary strode the quivering Broom with Carbonel balanced on the sadly diminished twigs behind her.

'Go on, say it!' he said. She took a deep breath and said:

> *If you please, my gallant Broom,*
> *Take us straight to John's bedroom.*

And the Broom, which had been giving little hops under her, as though it longed to take the air, rose smoothly and silently, circled once round the room and was away through the window. Rosemary gripped with her knees, and screwed up her eyes and her toes. But the motion was smooth and pleasant, and soon she dared to open her eyes and look around her. They were flying high. They skimmed the weather-cock of All Saints' Church, where she went on Sundays with her mother, they flew over the shopping centre, now empty and silent, with only here and there a lighted square of window, over the new housing estate and out over the moonlit country beyond. She was so fascinated by the shifting shapes beneath that she forgot to be frightened. The road wandered idly along, like a pale grey ribbon tossed there by some careless giant. Away to the south the river gleamed, a silver streak, and woods and houses, barns and ricks crouched like sleeping animals on the crazy paving that was the fields and meadows. Rosemary was so interested in watching it slip away from beneath her that she was quite surprised when Carbonel said, 'We're nearly there. Duck your head when we go in!'

She looked up, and there was Tussocks, apparently rising up to meet them with such speed that Rosemary had a queer feeling in her stomach. How on earth, of all those windows, could the broom be expected to know which was John's? But it sped on without any hesitation, and as it seemed that they must crash head on into the great castellated wall that rose in front of her, she flung herself flat along the broom and shut her eyes. But it was only by the light touch of a curtain brushing against her cheek that she knew they had passed into the room. There she was, actually on John's bed, with the broom beneath her. John shot up from the bedclothes, wide awake, with his hair standing up in spikes all over his head.

'Quick!' said Rosemary. 'Mount the broom behind me. We're going to the Law Giving to see Carbonel take possession of his kingdom!' To John's credit, he did not stop to ask questions. He tumbled out of bed, and all he said was:

'Whacko, budge up!'

Rosemary budged. It was rather a squash, but he bundled up behind her.

'Make haste!' said Carbonel. 'Now, the Town Hall roof, Rosemary.'

After a moment's thought she said:

On the Town Hall roof put us gently down,
And oblige John, Carbonel, and Rosemary Brown.

She was rather pleased with this, as being both polite and business-like.

'Duck!' shouted Carbonel.

And as they ducked the Broom swooshed through the window, and once more they were sailing through the night air back towards the town. They were not flying so high this time. John was bouncing up and down with excitement.

'Boy, oh boy! This is terrific! There's the Lodge and the gardener's cottage! That must be the railway by Spinnaker's wood!'

A train, like a jewelled snake, was threading its way through the darkness. A bat blundered into them and squeaked something.

'Don't mention it!' said Carbonel. And the bat flew off again. Soon they were over the first huddle of houses, and as they flew above the town the broom rose heavily. It was travelling more slowly now. The extra weight of John was telling on it. It skirted a tower here and a block of flats there, as though it was conserving its energy. As they drew nearer to the Town Hall they could see the stream of cats below them, still silently crowding in the same direction.

'It's a funny thing,' said Rosemary. 'Sometimes it looks like slates and bricks and roofs and chimneys, and sometimes like hills with grass and flowers and trees. It's difficult to see with the moon going behind the clouds every now and then.'

'I noticed that,' said John. 'Queer. But how could it be grass and trees, when we know it isn't?'

'How do you know it isn't?' asked Carbonel.

'Just look at the Town Hall roof!' interrupted John. They looked. It was a strange sight. The roof of the building in which Queen Elizabeth I had slept was covered with a thatch, not of straw, but of cats, and still more were pushing their way on from the surrounding buildings. So intent were the animals that they did not see the dark shape above them which was the broom.

'Where shall we land?' said Rosemary.

'What about behind that chimney?' said John.

The moon had gone behind a cloud again, and in the dim light they could not quite make out if it was a chimney stack with half a dozen different cowls and chimney pots, or a tree stump, with gnarled and twisted branches. But tree or chimney, behind it they could see and not be seen. The Broom alighted gently, and they found they were standing with their bare feet, not on cold slates, but on short, soft grass. Rosemary had lost her slippers some time ago. Before them a grassy slope fell steeply down towards a small flat valley, and both slope and valley were covered with cats.

'Look, they are all staring up at the clock!'

In the centre of the Town Hall roof was a four-sided clock. At each corner was a pillar which supported a small golden dome. Beneath the dome had once hung a bell which warned the town of fire and disaster and great happenings, both glad and sorry. The bell was now in the Fairfax Museum.

'I *thought* it was the clock,' said Rosemary in a puzzled way, 'but it can't be. It is a sort of little temple.'

'The throne of my fathers!' said Carbonel with emotion.

'Then you ought to be sitting there!' said John. 'Not that great cat that is there now!'

'A usurper!' hissed Carbonel. 'But he shall not remain there much longer!'

Sitting proudly under the golden dome was a huge ginger cat with a rabble of disreputable animals behind him.

'I say!' said John excitedly. 'I do believe ...'

'Hush, he's talking!' said Rosemary.

'Listen to me!' said the ginger cat.

There was a sighing murmur from the animals gazing up at him, and the rabble behind him pushed and jostled.

'Have you all brought your offerings, every cat and kitten among you?'

There was a murmur from the assembled cats.

'But sir,' said a voice from the front rank below, 'it is not possible for all cats to bring an offering. Many are poor and old ...'

'Silence!' spat the ginger cat, in a voice that made half the listening animals step back. 'If you are poor, others are not. There are larders and shop counters, are there not? Now, don't tell me you are going to be so simple as to tell me that you have no money, as though you are merely humans. A pounce, a spring when their backs are turned and the herring, the chicken, or whatever it is is yours!

'My Court,' he turned and indicated the grinning animals behind him, 'my Court and I shall not ask where you bring the offerings from, so long as they are there. But bring them you must!'

'This is frightful!' muttered Carbonel. 'Far worse than I ever dreamed. Here at the Law Giving to incite them to rob and steal!'

'But look here!' said John again. 'I am quite sure it is ...'

But the ginger cat was speaking again, and Carbonel said, 'Hush!'

'Come forward any animal who has been foolish enough to come without an offering!' went on the ginger animal in a voice that was soft, but so wicked that it froze the marrow in their bones.

A dozen cats cringed forward. Most of them were very old or very young.

'So many?' went on their tormentor, with mock sympathy. 'What a pity. Well, you know what to expect. Or is this perhaps a gesture of defiance? Is there anyone here foolish enough to dispute my right to be a leader among you?' He was standing now, looking down on them, a magnificent animal.

There was a sound from the assembled cats, half sigh and half murmur, but not one of them spoke. For a brief second Carbonel waited. Then, mounting one of the gnarled branches of the tree ... or was it a chimney cowl? ... his challenge rang out over the roof-tops.

'I do!'

There was a pause and a stir while every animal turned to look towards the voice that had hurled defiance. Hundreds of pairs of yellow eyes gazed up at them.

'And who are you?' sneered the ginger cat when he had recovered from his surprise.

'I am Carbonel X, your king by right of birth.'

There was an excited murmur among the assembled animals.

'Silence, you rabble!' hissed the ginger cat, and the murmur died.

'So you are Carbonel X. You lie; seven years ago he disappeared into thin air, and has never been heard of since.'

'My Lord!' said the old voice that had spoken up before. 'My Lord, there is an ancient prophecy among our people:

> *A kit among the stars shall sit,*
> *Beyond the aid of feline wit.*
> *Empty Royal throne and mat*
> *Till three Queens save a princely cat.*

John and Rosemary could see the speaker now, a gaunt old tabby cat.

'It is Malkin, my father's faithful adviser and friend,' whispered Carbonel.

'Still harping on that foolish nursery rhyme, my good Malkin!'

The ginger cat laughed a horrid, jeering laugh, and the disreputable mob he called his Court nudged one another and joined in.

'If it is the Prince, my Lord, he can prove it,' went on Malkin anxiously. 'He will have the three royal, snow-white hairs in the end of his tail.'

Rosemary forgot that she was supposed to be keeping out of sight. She jumped up from behind the tree ... or chimney stack ... and, waving the broom to attract attention, she called out:

'He really has got three white hairs at the end of his tail – I've often noticed them!'

'So, ho! You have brought your young witch with you!' jeered the ginger cat. 'Or are you still tied to her apron strings?'

'I'm not a witch,' said Rosemary indignantly, 'and I never wear an apron, except to wash up! He is abso-lutely free. I bought him with my three Queens, and then I undid the Silent Magic, and set him free for ever!'

'It is perfectly true – I saw it all happen!' John shouted, popping out from the other side of the chimney ... or tree.

The cats below raised a murmur that the ginger tyrant could not quell this time. Rosemary saw their glowing eyes switch backwards and forwards from them to the ginger cat, as each spoke in turn. She could see the enemy cat was sitting down once more, motionless except for the twitching at the end of his tail. John sud-denly whispered urgently to her:

'I say, where have the Alley Cats gone to? There were dozens of them standing behind the little temple, and now I can only see about half a dozen of them.' But Carbonel had eyes for no one but the ginger cat, who had risen to his feet. 'Keep watch behind you,' he said quietly, then his voice rang out over the roof-tops: 'Who is for Carbonel the King? For law and order? For peace and plenty?'

Someone shouted 'Carbonel for ever!' and the mass of cats heaved uncertainly for a minute, then half of them surged towards Carbonel, some of the others slunk towards the ginger cat, and the remainder hovered uncertainly between. The ginger cat stood motionless, but his flattened ears showed how angry he was. The six remaining Alley Cats closed in behind him.

'Listen to me!' he snarled, 'common, black witch's cat! I am Leader here by right of conquest. If anyone dares to dispute my leadership, let him fight for it!' He arched his bristling back and hurled a wailing challenge to the stars. Carbonel yawned deliberately. Then he stepped delicately down, his silky body gleaming in the moonlight. Some of the cats closed in behind him, but without taking his eyes off his enemy he said: 'Stand back, my people. This is between the two of us alone.' He moved slowly and deliberately into the little arena at the foot of the slope.

24

The battle

As Carbonel made his way towards his enemy the animals drew back and made way for him to pass. The ginger cat was waiting for him. They stood facing each other, backs arched and bristling, hurling strange, blood-curdling taunts at each other.

John was jumping up and down and shouting, 'Go it, Carbonel!' and 'Oh boy, oh boy!'

Rosemary felt something furry rub against her bare ankle. It was Malkin.

'Dear Madam!' he said. 'Can you do nothing to help with your magic arts? If only the tyrant would disappear there would be an end to our troubles. The Alley Cats can do nothing without a leader. Can't you make him vanish in a puff of smoke, or turn him into a toad, or perhaps a mouse?'

'But I have no magic arts!' said Rosemary. The old cat sighed.

'What a pity. Then all we can do is to try to see fair play. I do not trust that ginger fiend. He will stop at nothing to gain his ends.'

'Couldn't we stop them fighting somehow?' said Rosemary anxiously.

'No. That would do no good, even if we could,' said Malkin. 'It would only put off the battle to another time ... and blood is as red tomorrow as today.'

'Besides, I'm sure Carbonel would hate us to interfere,' said John. 'Look at him now!'

The two cats were stalking round each other very

slowly with bristling backs, hurling strange cat insults at each other. Then they stood motionless, nose to nose, spitting defiance.

'Go it, Carbonel!' shouted John. 'Don't you see, Rosie? He has got to beat that ginger brute in single combat. Though what Aunt Amabel would say, I can't imagine.'

'But why should Mrs Pendlebury Parker say anything?' asked Rosemary absently. The cats were sparring and hissing at each other, as John described it, 'like a couple of pressure cookers'.

'Why should Aunt Amabel mind? Well, after all, it is her long lost Popsey Dinkums.'

'What!' gasped Rosemary, 'are you sure? Good gracious, why didn't you tell me?'

'I'm absolutely certain. I'd know him anywhere. And I did try to tell you, but you wouldn't listen.'

Her attention had left the fight for a minute, but at that moment the two cats sprang at each other, rolling over and over, locked together.

'Oh dear,' said Rosemary miserably, 'I do wish they did not have to do it!' And she covered her eyes with her hands.

The cats were rolling over and over now, biting and thrusting with their hind claws. They parted, and once more stood, noses almost touching.

'Oh, poor Carbonel. He is bleeding!' Although Rosemary had covered her eyes with her hands, she could not resist separating her fingers, so that she could see what was going on. Carbonel had a great gash on his flank.

'Look at your King now!' jeered the ginger cat. 'Bleeding like every animal who dares to defy me; bleeding and limping into the bargain! Come on, my witch's cat!' and he danced triumphantly round Carbonel, who stood his ground, motionless except for his threshing tail. Five times they sprang at each other, rolling over and over in a flurry of fur, sometimes one uppermost and sometimes the other. The watching cats surged silently backwards and forwards as the fighters shifted their battle-ground.. The sixth time, a cloud covered the moon so that the children could only see a dark, tumbling mass. John leapt up and down with anxiety, and Rosemary chewed the end of one of her pigtails, a thing she had not done since she was a little girl.

'Oh dear, what is happening?' she said in an agony of suspense. It seemed hours before the moon came out again, but when at last the roof-tops were flooded once more with pale light, Carbonel was standing, panting, over the prostrate body of the ginger cat. It was true he was standing on three legs, but there was no doubt at all who was the victor. Carbonel threw up his scratched and bleeding head and called:

'Who is your leader now by right of conquest?' And the great assembly sent up a wailing cry:

'You are, O Carbonel! You are!'

The defeated ginger cat said nothing, but he moved his head restlessly from side to side.

'Oh, be careful, master!' called Malkin. 'Do not trust him!' But his frail old voice was blown away by the little breeze that had sprung up.

Carbonel had turned his back on his enemy, shaking each paw in turn, and as he made his way, limping, up the slope to the little temple, the animals drew respectfully back to let him pass. All eyes were on Carbonel, and nobody noticed that the little knot of Alley Cats had disappeared, but just as the black cat was about to mount the steps at the base of the throne, John suddenly yelled:

'Look behind you!'

And as he shouted the Alley Cats flung themselves on the unsuspecting Carbonel. Had he not had that second's warning he would have had no chance at all, but he whipped round just in time to present the on-coming animals with bared teeth and claws. At the same moment from behind the ridge yet another knot of animals leapt on him from behind.

'You cowards!' yelled Rosemary.

'Yes, by gum you are!' shouted John. 'Carbonel won his battle, and he is leader by right of conquest!'

'He can't fight all those Alley Cats single-pawed,' said Malkin. 'Look where the ginger tyrant is egging them on!'

But Carbonel was not alone. Pandemonium had broken loose as more and more animals hurled them-selves into the battle, on one side or the other, while from the vantage point of the far ridge the ginger cat urged them on. Carbonel had disappeared under an avalanche of struggling cats.

'Can nobody remove that ginger fiend?' wailed Malkin.

'John,' said Rosemary. 'Do you think the broom could take us all three to Tussocks? If only we could manage it, of course.'

'It's worth trying,' said John.

'Darling broom!' said Rosemary. 'I simply can't say it all in rhyme this time, but when this is all over I will make it into a real poem, a saga, the sort of thing that is told to your children and their children's children, I promise faithfully. But we must do something quickly to save Carbonel, or it will be too late. Please take us up, John and me, and circle over the battle ...' John in-terrupted:

'You had better give me your dressing gown, Rosie.'

'And when I say "Down", drop like a stone, and John will throw the dressing gown over the ginger cat and scoop him up.'

'And when she says "Up!" rise at once and circle again.'

'And then we had better see what happens next. If you will do all this I will never ask you to do anything again!'

'Hurry!' said Malkin. 'My poor young master!'

Below them was a swaying mass of cats. Only a few, too old or too infirm, or too young, were not engaged in the battle. Rosemary was pulling off her dressing gown. Then she straddled the broom with John behind her. It was not easy to mount because the broom hopped so impatiently up and down.

'Heaven prosper you!' said Malkin, as they rose slowly from the roof.

'Good-bye!' called Rosemary. 'Look after Carbonel! Now, Broom, circle round where the battle is fiercest. I can't see the ginger cat anywhere, John, and it's all very well to talk about "scooping" him up, but I don't see how it's to be done!'

The children peered anxiously into the writhing mass beneath them, made even more indistinct by a haze of flying fur. There was no sign of either Carbonel or the ginger cat.

'Look there!' said John, and he pointed to the little temple; and there, by the side of it, sat the ginger tyrant, licking his hurts and grinning at the boiling mass of fighting animals below. John gripped the broom handle with his knees and held the dressing gown with both hands.

'I'm ready, Rosie! Look out for the lurch when we pick him up!'

Rosemary nodded.

'One, two, three, down!' she said, and swiftly and silently the broom swooped. John dropped the thick folds of the dressing gown over the unsuspecting cat. Caught entirely unawares, it fought and struggled in the hampering folds, but John held grimly on.

'I've got him, Rosie. We had better get away as quickly as possible. I'll tie him up with the dressing gown cord as we go along, for safety.'

'Up, Broom!' called Rosemary, and nearly shot over the handle as, with a sickening lurch, the over-loaded broom rose heavily into the sky.

'Look up, you Alley Cats!' called John. 'Look at your proud leader now!'

The moon had gone behind a cloud again, and as first one and then another pair of jewelled eyes peered up at them from the darkness, the sound of fighting faltered and died. And when the moon came out again there was not a sound to be heard, and every animal in that great assembly was staring up at them, where John held up the ginger cat for them to see, trussed like a chicken with the dressing gown cord.

'Who is your Leader by right of birth and conquest?' And the cats below cried, 'Carbonel, Carbonel is our leader!'

'That's all very well,' whispered Rosemary, 'but where is Carbonel?'

'Don't worry, Rosie, I saw him throw off a pile of cats just now. He looked shaky but determined. I say, look at the temple!'

Rosemary looked. Underneath the golden dome, sitting on the throne of his fathers, was Carbonel. The broom circled round the temple, and he gazed up.

'Good-bye, Carbonel! We are taking him back where he belongs!' called Rosemary.

'He could never hold up his head here again in any case, and Aunt Amabel will be thrilled to have him back again!'

Carbonel gazed up at them with his great golden eyes.

'Farewell! Farewell, my faithful friends! And the gratitude of a king go with you!'

And as the broom turned and headed towards the country, they heard a triumphant cry which grew fainter and fainter as the Town Hall faded into the distance.

'Long live King Carbonel! Long live King Carbonel!'

25

The end

THE broom skimmed off obediently at Rosemary's request.

'Oh, no you don't, my Popsey Dinkum!' said John, as the ginger cat renewed his struggles. 'And that is not at all the sort of language that Aunt Amabel likes to hear!'

At the mention of Mrs Pendlebury Parker the animal mewed pitifully.

'Well, thank goodness he is able to struggle so hard,' said Rosemary. 'It shows that he can't be very badly hurt. I say, John, we're flying awfully low.'

John had been so busy with his bundle of cat and dressing gown that he had had no time for anything else. They were flying over the new building estate at the edge of the town now, barely skimming the chimney pots. Once Rosemary banged her leg on a lightning conductor.

'I've noticed that when the moon is shining clearly, it seems to gain height.'

'I should think that the poor thing is completely worn out. It has been tremendously plucky all evening, and now it has got this hefty great weight to carry.'

Rosemary patted the broom gently. It was warm and damp beneath her fingers like an over-ridden horse.

'Please do your best, dear Broom! You have been so splendid, but I know the last bus has gone, and we couldn't walk all these miles, not with bare feet we couldn't.'

The broom seemed to shake itself; then it rose a little higher. Luckily the moon came out again, and it seemed to take fresh heart. They made steady progress for some distance, but by the time they had reached the Lodge of Tussocks the broom had barely strength enough to clear the gate. The trees on either side of the drive were thick and tall and very little moonlight found its way beneath them. It struggled bravely on, but beneath her anxious fingers Rosemary could feel its pulse beat uncertainly, and several times John, who was fully occupied with his bundle, felt his bare feet drag painfully on the gravelled drive. When they came to a bend in the drive the broom seemed uncertain of its direction and went blindly on towards the rhododendrons. If it had not been for Rosemary's guiding hand it would have blundered into the shrubbery.

'Shall we get off and walk?' asked Rosemary. 'We're nearly there.'

Indeed, Tussocks was in sight, huge and dark except for one single light. But the gallant broom shook itself once more. They could feel it gather itself together for one last effort. Steadily it sped on over the final hundred yards, head up and its few remaining twigs only occasionally dragging on the ground, to fall with a clatter on the top step of the broad flight that led to the front door.

'Good old Broom!' said John, and stooped to pat it as it lay panting on the ground.

'I say, Rosie,' said John suddenly. 'What on earth are we going to say to Aunt Amabel?'

But Rosemary was already hanging on to the great wrought-iron door-bell and ringing with all her might. Not until she heard it clanging in the distance did she realize that arriving in the middle of the night in their

'Farewell! Farewell, my faithful friends!'

night things with the missing cat rolled up in a dressing
gown, would need a great deal of explaining.

'You owl!' said John.

'Owl yourself!' said Rosemary. But there was no
time for a 'you're another' kind of argument, for the
light above the door was switched on, and after the
bolts had been shot back the door was cautiously
opened, and there stood Chambers, the butler, in a
purple dressing gown.

'H ... hallo, Chambers!' said John, as airily as he
could. 'It's me and Rosemary Brown. Do let us in. It's
a bit cold out here in nothing but pyjamas.'

'Master Lancelot, you naughty boy! Whatever are
you doing out at this time of night, and in your night
things, too?'

'Well,' said John slowly. 'It's like this ...' But a voice
from the stairs interrupted. It was Mrs Pendlebury
Parker.

'What is it Chambers?' she asked, and then she saw
John. 'Lancelot, come here at once! Out at one o'clock
in the morning and not even properly dressed! And
Rosemary in her nightdress! What is the meaning of
this?'

'I am very sorry we are out so late,' said Rosemary,
'but we have brought back your Popsey Dinkums. We
rescued him from a fight. He is wrapped up in my dressing gown.'

John was already undoing the cord, and unceremoni-
ously unrolling the cat.

'My Popsey Dinkums!' shrieked Mrs Pendlebury
Parker, as the battle-scarred animal emerged. 'What
have the nasty rough cats been doing to you?' And she
fell on her knees and hugged the dishevelled animal to
her pink satin dressing gown. Then she looked up at the

children. 'My dear Lancelot, I don't know what you have been up to, but if you have brought me back my darling Popsey Dinkums I cannot be cross. But what about Mrs Brown? Rosemary, I cannot believe that your mother knows anything about this!'

'No, I'm afraid she doesn't. I'm afraid I didn't think. I just ...' She broke off. Suddenly she felt that the only thing that mattered was that she should be able to lie down and go to sleep.

'Well, we can't disturb her at one o'clock in the morning. It would frighten her out of her wits. We must ring her up first thing before she has time to discover you are not there. What time does she usually get up?'

'About seven, as a rule,' said Rosemary faintly.

'Good gracious me! The child is falling asleep on her feet. Chambers, you had better put her in the pink room, and we will discuss it in the morning. And my darling Dinkums shall have his very own blue cushion to sleep on, and some chicken, he shall! Chopped up very fine, Chambers, don't forget.'

'Very good. madam,' said Chambers, with disapproval of the whole affair oozing from him.

Rosemary had a dim memory afterwards of having been carried upstairs and put into a huge bed, and the next thing she knew it was broad daylight, and John was shaking her arm.

'Wake up, Rosie! It's after eight o'clock. Look here, what did we do with the broom last night?' Rosemary sat up.

'Goodness, I forgot all about it. We must have left it on the door-step. How could we have been so ungrateful?'

'Well, come on, let's go and look.'

She was just going to jump out of bed when she suddenly remembered something.

'But John, I've no clothes to put on. I can't go about in my nightie!'

'It's all right. I've brought you a pair of shorts of mine and a shirt ... Buck up and put them on and I'll tell you what has been going on. You know, Aunt Amabel is a good sort, really. She rang up your mother before she had time to discover that you were not there, and she got her to promise that she would not be angry with you because we brought back her beastly Dinkums.' Rosemary felt a great wave of relief, because how could she possibly explain it all even to the most understanding of mothers? 'And that isn't all,' went on John. 'She says that you and I must share the reward she offered!'

'Gracious!' said Rosemary. 'I had forgotten that there was a reward.' She had put on the shirt and shorts and was watching with interest the three different views of herself brushing her hair that she could see in the great three-sided mirror. The brushes had gleaming silver backs with initials on them.

'It will be twenty-five pounds each,' said John. Rosemary dropped the brushes and gasped. 'I can see you with your mouth open three times over in that looking glass – you do look funny! Buck up, we have just time to look for the broom before breakfast.'

They ran downstairs together and out of the front door, but there was no sign of the broom where they had left it on the door-step. An old man in a green apron was sweeping up some leaves from the drive. John hailed him.

'I say, Wilson. Did you see an old broom here on the steps this morning?'

'No, Master Lance, there weren't no broom. Only an old stick that might have been the handle of one.'

'What did you do with it?'

'Bless you, I put it on the bonfire behind the tool shed, not ten minutes ago.'

'Quick!' said John. 'We might be in time to save it!'

They ran faster than they had ever run before, round to the other side of the house, along the terrace, through the rose garden to the tool shed, which was at the far end of the kitchen garden. But they were too late. As they reached the bonfire a shower of sparks of every colour of the rainbow shot up from the glowing heart, but there was no sign of the broom handle, only a handful of glowing wood ash.

'Good-bye, Broom!' said Rosemary softly, 'and thank you.' And as if in reply a little puff of smoke wreathed its way up and was gone. The children walked in silence back to the house.

'There is a letter for you, Master Lance,' said the maid who brought in their breakfast. It was scrambled egg and sausages, which was the nicest breakfast that Rosemary could have chosen. But she sat looking at her plate with unseeing eyes. It was all over. Even if she ever saw Carbonel again, without the broom she could never hear him talking to her. She felt she ought to be feeling pleased at the success of all their plans, but all she could feel was that everything had gone flat and dull. John would be going home and there would be no more Tussocks. Her gloomy thoughts were interrupted by John, who was reading his letter.

'I say, Rosie. My mother says that when I go home next week we are going to the sea, because of my sister being peaky after measles, and she says would you like to come home with me and go with us? Would your mother let you?'

'Would you let me, Mummy?' said Rosemary, when a bewildered Mrs Brown arrived, 'or would you be too lonely?'

Her mother smiled. 'I shall be far too busy to be lonely.'

'More sides to middling?' asked Rosemary sympathetically.

'Not this time, darling – moving house!'

'Moving house? Are we leaving Tottenham Grove?'

Her mother smiled again. 'You are not the only person to spring surprises! I had a letter this morning from Mr Featherstone, the man that for some reason you and John call the Occupier. He has offered us a flat in his house, unfurnished, so that we can have all our own furniture again.'

'But Mummy, can we afford it?'

'I think we can, because instead of paying him rent he wants me to be Wardrobe Mistress of the Netherley Players. That will still leave me plenty of time to do my own work as well. What do you think of that?'

I am sure I need not tell you what Rosemary thought, because if you have read her adventures as far as this I am quite sure you will know.

When she returned from her holiday with John and his family, looking so brown that her mother barely knew her, it was to their new home, with all their own familiar furniture to welcome them like old friends. One of the first visitors they had was a magnificent black cat with three white hairs at the end of his tail. Of course it was Carbonel, and although she could no longer hear him talking he purred so loudly that there was not much doubt what he meant.

Rosemary kept her promise to the broom, and wrote the whole story as a ballad, which she had accepted for the school magazine. As for Mrs Cantrip, without her book of magic she became quite clean and respectable. Rosemary persuaded Miss Maggie to give her a job as washer-up. The last time I had tea at the Copper Kettle, that thriving tea-shop, she was still there, and giving every satisfaction.

BARBARA SLEIGH (1906–1982) worked for the BBC Children's Hour and is the author of *Carbonel* and two sequels: *The Kingdom of Carbonel* and *Carbonel and Calidor*.